After the Vows

D.E. Haggerty

Copyright © 2024 D.E. Haggerty

All rights reserved.

D.E. Haggerty asserts the moral right to be identified as the author of this work.

ISBN: 9789083465517

After the Vows is a work of fiction. The names, characters, places, and incidents portrayed in it are the product of the author's imagination. Any resemblance to actual persons, living or dead, events or locations is entirely coincidental.

All rights reserved. No part of this publication may be reproduced, stored in a retrieval system, or transmitted, in any form or by any means, electronic, mechanical, photocopying, recording or otherwise, without the prior permission of the author.

No portion of this book may be reproduced in any form without written permission from the publisher or author, except as permitted by U.S. copyright law.

Also by D.E. Haggerty

Before It Was Love
How to Date a Rockstar
How to Love a Rockstar
How to Fall For a Rockstar
How to Be a Rockstar's Girlfriend
How to Catch a Rockstar
My Forever Love
Forever For You
Just For Forever
Stay For Forever
Only Forever
Meet Disaster
Meet Not
Meet Dare
Meet Hate
Bragg's Truth
Bragg's Love
Perfect Bragg
Bragg's Match
Bragg's Christmas

A Hero for Hailey
A Protector for Phoebe
A Soldier for Suzie
A Fox for Faith
A Christmas for Chrissie
A Valentine for Valerie
A Love for Lexi
About Face
At Arm's Length
Hands Off
Knee Deep
Molly's Misadventures

Chapter 1

Chloe – a woman who doesn't believe the customer is always right

CHLOE

A customer sidles up to the bar. I smile at him. "What can I get you?"

"I'll have a Summer Ale and your phone number."

I roll my eyes. If I had a dime for every time a customer hit on me, I could make a large ball of metal and throw it at every customer who thinks it's okay to hit on a woman just because she's serving you alcohol.

"One Summer Ale coming up." I pour the beer and set it on the bar in front of the customer. "That'll be five dollars."

He waves a ten-dollar bill at me. "You can have this if you give me your phone number."

Am I supposed to be impressed? "No thanks."

"Come on, darling." He motions to the bar and restaurant. "You must want more in life than this."

Wrong. I'm living the dream. This bar and restaurant is part of *Five Fathoms Brewing*, the brewery I co-founded with my four best friends – Maya, Paisley, Nova, and Sophia.

Maya came up with the idea of founding a brewery. Paisley experimented with brewing beer. Nova started selling it to other restaurants on the island of Smuggler's Hideaway where we all grew up. And Sophia helped fund the project. The rest is history.

I snatch the bill from him. "I'm good. I'll get your change."

"I don't want the change. I want your telephone number."

"It's good to want things." I set his change on the bar and start to walk toward another customer. He leans over the bar and grasps my arm to stop me. I glare at his hand. "If you want to keep your hand, you'll release my arm."

"What's a little thing like you going to do?"

Little thing? I'm five-foot-nine. The furthest thing from little.

I scrunch my nose and pretend to consider his question. "Probably break your fingers. Or maybe your wrist? What kind of work do you do? What would hinder you most? The inability to use your fingers or your wrist?"

He barks out a laugh. "You're cute."

"I warned you," I sing as I reach for his hand.

A waitress slams her serving tray down on the bar. "Chloe!"

"Hey, Addy."

"Do not break his fingers."

"Why not?" I pout.

"It's bad for business."

I glance around the bar and restaurant. The place is packed as usual. "I think we're doing okay."

Addy narrows her eyes at me. "I'll tell Nova, Maya, and Paisley."

"Tattletale," I mutter before releasing the man's hand. "Fine. You can go."

"I'm going to sue you!" he yells as he shakes out his hand.

"Don't be a baby."

He snarls at me. "You're deranged."

I bow. "Thank you very much."

He backs away. "This place is crazy."

"Don't forget your beer!" I holler after him.

He rushes out of the door. I shake my head. "Will men never learn?"

"Learn what?" the bartender, Theo, asks as he joins me behind the bar.

I untie the apron from around my waist. "I guess it's time for me to get back to doing next week's schedule."

He moans. "You're not answering my question, which means you scared another customer away."

"When I arrived," Addy says, "she had him in a chokehold."

"Exaggerate much? I bent his finger back a tiny bit. No snapping involved."

She sighs. "You're a menace."

I grin. "Thank you."

I check that no one on the restaurant floor needs me before making my way to my office. I'd rather work behind the bar, but I really do need to get next week's schedule finished and the inventory ordered. Being the bar and restaurant manager of *Five Fathoms* is not as much fun as I expected.

I barely have a chance to switch on my computer before my door flies open and Nova, Maya, and Paisley rush inside.

"Addy's a tattletale."

"It's not tattling when she's not revealing secrets," Paisley says.

I salute her. "Thank you, nerd girl, for correcting me."

"I know you're being sarcastic but I don't care if you call me a nerd girl."

Of course, she doesn't. Paisley is proud of being a nerd. I give her a hard time about it but if I were as smart as she is, I'd be proud of myself, too. There's a reason she's the one in charge of developing new beers for *Five Fathoms* and I'm the one working in the restaurant.

Nova sighs. "Can we stick to the matter at hand? You can't be getting into fights with the customers."

Uh oh. Miss Optimistic is frowning. She must be really annoyed. Miss Sunshine hardly ever frowns. It's why she's the sales manager for *Five Fathoms*. When someone tells her no, she keeps smiling and pushing until she makes the sale. She can sell fish to a mermaid.

"I think there's been a misunderstanding. I didn't hurt the customer."

"But he's claiming he's going to sue," Maya says.

"He's not going to sue. His claim is fictional. Something you should understand."

Maya is the definition of a bookworm. If it weren't for us, she'd probably hide away in her home with her books all the time.

Even with us around, she tries to get out of leaving her house. She claims she can do her work as the financial manager for *Five Fathoms* at her dining room table. She's crazy if she thinks we'll allow her to become a hermit.

"Whether he sues or not, is irrelevant. You can't go around hurting customers," Paisley declares.

"Why not?"

"Because you don't want to get arrested," Nova says.

"Again," Maya mutters.

I wave away their concerns. "I won't get arrested. I have an 'in' with the police."

Paisley slides her glasses up her nose. "I don't think Sophia will appreciate you using her brother to get out of trouble."

"Good thing Sophia's not here then, isn't it?" I fire back.

Although Sophia is one of the original founders of *Five Fathoms,* she doesn't live on the island with us. She's a hotshot marketing exec in Atlanta now.

Maya clears her throat. "But she will be soon."

Ah, yes. Sophia isn't a hotshot in Atlanta anymore. She got fired from her job because some asshole stole her work. I volunteered to give him a lesson in stealing but Sophia said she was moving back to Smuggler's Hideaway.

"I can't wait for her to come home." I rub my hands together as I imagine all the fun times we'll have. "She's been away too long."

Maya sighs. "I can't wait until she falls in love."

I frown. "This is not some romance book. Sophia is not going to fall in love with the man who caused her to flee the island in the first place."

Sophia didn't merely leave Smuggler's Hideaway. She fled when the boy she was crushing on humiliated her. It's a long story but it's her story to tell.

Paisley clears her throat. "Let's make sure there is a company for Sophia to work for when she returns."

I roll my eyes. "*Five Fathoms Brewing* will be here. Some asshole who thinks it's okay to grab a woman when she refuses to give him her phone number isn't going to destroy us."

"Chloe's beauty strikes another man down," Nova says.

I lock my limbs to stop myself from flinching at the word beauty. I don't want to be beautiful. I don't want anything to do with beauty. Beauty is the only thing my mother cared about.

And the lengths she went to, to ensure I was thin – because only thin people are beautiful in her opinion – still give me nightmares.

"I'm not beautiful," I deny and Nova immediately backpedals.

"Sorry, Chloe."

I wave away her excuse. My friends know all about my mom. Mostly. There's no reason to bring up the past. It's dead and buried.

"I need to get the schedule for next week finished."

Paisley steps toward the door. "We'll let you return to your work."

She leaves and Nova follows her. Maya shuffles toward me.

"Are you okay?"

"I'm fine. Customers can be assholes. It's part of the job if you're working as a bartender."

She bites her bottom lip as she hesitates. Maya is a shy thing. We've known each other for twenty-five years. We've been through our first periods together, our first kisses together, and numerous heartbreaks together. But still. She's hesitant.

"What is it?"

"I want to make sure you're not feeling sad after being reminded of your mom."

I force a smile on my face. Thinking about my mom doesn't make me sad. It makes me mad. But Maya doesn't understand. She still yearns for the love of her family despite how they treated her.

"I promise I'm okay Maya."

"Mermaid promise?" Mermaids are considered sacred on Smuggler's Hideaway. Breaking a mermaid promise is one of the worst things you can do.

I nod. "Mermaid promise."

I wait until she's gone to collapse in my chair. I wasn't lying to her. I am okay. I'll always be okay. Chloe Summers will not let life get her down.

Chapter 2

Lucas – a man whose arrival on Smuggler's Hideaway will cause heads to turn and hearts to yearn

LUCAS

"You have arrived at your destination."

I scowl at the GPS. I'm in the middle of nowhere. This can't be my destination. I check the address I typed into the GPS. It's correct – 5 Treasure Trail in the town of Smuggler's Rest.

Damnit. Did I get catfished?

This is what I get for renting a house sight unseen. I should have known better when the address was Treasure Trail. I should have gone house hunting when I was on the island to interview for my position as a police officer on Smuggler's Hideaway. But I didn't want to be away from my daughter any longer than necessary.

Natalia is twelve and pushing for her independence but I need to protect her. After her mother – my ex-wife Holly – abandoned us, I don't want her to ever feel as if I've abandoned her. I wouldn't. Natalia is my world.

She's at a tennis camp this week, which gives me the chance to get us settled into our new house. She's not happy about moving but I couldn't live any longer in the city where everyone looked at me and my girl with pity. I'm hoping that presenting her with a brand-new teenage girl's dream bedroom will help smooth the transition.

I dig my phone out of the cup holder and dial the real estate agent.

"You have reached Buccaneer Rental Agency. We're closed for the weekend. We're happy to answer your enquiries when we return to work on Monday morning. Have a lovely weekend."

Fat lot of good the rental agency is. I type the address into the map app on my phone.

"Shit," I swear when the map app shows I'm at the exact location of the house.

I throw the phone onto the seat before doing a U-turn and heading back toward the town of Smuggler's Rest. It's a small town. I can find Treasure Trail without the GPS.

I take the first left when I arrive in town. I scowl when I notice none of the streets I cross have street signs. Maybe moving here was a mistake after all.

I pull my truck into a parking lot. I better ask for directions or I'll be driving around town all day and night.

The parking lot is packed, but I manage to nab a spot in the rear. When I step out of my truck, the music hits me. What is this place? *Five Fathoms Brewing.* There's a brewery on this small island?

The door slams open and a man stomps outside. I step to the side before he crashes into me.

"I wouldn't go in there. The bartender's a bitch."

He keeps going before I get a chance to ask him what happened. It's none of my business, I remind myself. I'm not on duty.

I enter the building. It's an old barn, which has been renovated with wide wooden floors, stained wooden beams, and big glass doors looking out over the dunes to the ocean beyond.

A waitress immediately approaches me. "Did he bother you?"

"Who bother me?"

She waves toward outside. "The jerk who stomped out of here all mad claiming he was going to sue us."

"Oh him. He didn't bother me."

She blows out a breath. "Good. He grabbed one of the owners when she wouldn't give him her phone number. When she fought back, he got mad."

I frown. "Was she injured? Do you need the police? I'm a police officer."

"You are? Where?"

"Here."

Technically, I haven't begun my job yet but I will soon.

"Here? As in the island of Smuggler's Hideaway?"

"Yes."

She giggles. "Nice try. I know all of the police officers on this island. You aren't one of them."

I hold out my hand. "I'm Lucas Fellows, the newest police officer on the island."

Understanding lights in her eyes. "I'm Addy. Nice to meet you."

"Now you know I'm legit. Is the owner okay?

"Chloe's fine. You can see for yourself." Addy points to the woman standing at the mouth of the hallway.

No wonder the customer asked this woman out. She's a complete knockout with her porcelain skin and shiny auburn hair. She's tall, slender, and elegant. She should be on the cover of one of those fancy magazines my ex used to buy in bulk.

She's wearing shorts and I can't get enough of those long legs. I bet they'd feel wonderful wrapped around my hips. My cock twitches in agreement.

I clear my throat and force thoughts of Chloe's legs out of my mind. I'm not getting involved with a woman when the ink on my divorce papers is still fresh. Besides, my focus has to be on my daughter, Natalia, now. My needs can wait.

"Do you want a table? Will anyone be joining you?"

"Nah. I'm not staying. I need directions to Treasure Trail."

She grins. "Treasure Trail?"

"Please tell me I haven't been catfished."

She pats my hand. "Don't you worry. Treasure Trail exists and I think I know what house you're moving into."

Her amusement has the hairs on my neck rising. What's funny? Is the house I rented some kind of haunted house? Or derelict? Crap. Natalia's joining me in a week. I need the house finished before she arrives.

She steers me toward the door. "I'll give you directions."

I worry her directions are some kind of ruse considering the looney smile on her face but I arrive at the house I recognize from the pictures the realtor sent me five minutes later. It's not derelict. And if it happens to be haunted, I'll hire a witch to get rid of any paranormal presence.

I dig out the keys the realtor sent me. Time to figure out if I need to search for a witch.

I climb up the stairs to the porch and unlock the door. The scent of lemon hits me the second I enter. Good. The extra two hundred dollars I paid for a cleaning crew was worth it.

The living room has an oversized L-shaped sofa facing a large television perfect for watching football on. Beyond the living room is the kitchen. It's separated from the living room by an island with four chairs at it. Off to the side is a kitchen nook.

I'm curious about the backyard. I open the French doors and step out onto the back deck. The area is fenced in. Perfect for a dog.

I've always wanted one, but Holly claimed she was allergic. She wasn't allergic. She was afraid a dog would claim my attention. My ex-wife needed to be the center of attention at all times. Which is impossible when you're a police officer working shifts in a big city.

Ever since Holly left, Natalia's been begging for a dog. I haven't given in yet, but I plan for one of our first excursions on Smuggler's Hideaway to be a trip to the pound to pick out a new pet.

I step back inside the house and climb the stairs to check on the bedrooms. There are three bedrooms and two bathrooms. I pick out a room for Natalia before returning to my truck to start bringing in the boxes.

I rented the house furnished but there's still a lot to unpack – kitchenware, sheets, towels – and then there's Natalia's stuff. I admit, I might be spoiling her a bit much since her mom left us.

I nearly have my truck empty when a woman pedals by on a bicycle. She turns into the driveway next door and parks her bike before removing her helmet. She shakes out her auburn hair and…

Fuck.

No wonder the waitress at the brewery was laughing when she gave me directions to my house. She knew my new neighbor would be none other than her boss, Chloe.

I can't look away as Chloe struts to the front door of her house. Her pert little ass jiggles as she moves and I groan.

If I didn't have Natalia, I wouldn't hesitate to march on over there and introduce myself. I bet it wouldn't be long before Chloe and I were rolling around getting sweaty in her sheets.

But I can't. I'm not against one-night stands but I can't have one with my new neighbor. How awkward would it be when she wanted more and I refused? I don't need to introduce my daughter to that kind of drama.

My cock disagrees. He's on board with drama as long as at the end of the night he can bury himself between Chloe's creamy thighs.

It's not happening. My priority is and always will be my daughter.

I can resist the temptation of my new neighbor.

Chapter 3

Humiliation – when the sexy cop next door wants nothing to do with you

C*HLOE*

"All right, Addy. Let's see what the big deal is about my new neighbor."

The waitress couldn't wait to tell me a hot guy was moving into the house next door to mine. Not merely a hot guy but also a police officer. She knows I have a thing for men in uniform.

I pause with my hand on my doorknob when I notice a man run past my house. Holy mermaid tails. Is this the man my waitress was panting over?

I get what the big deal is. He's wearing shorts and shoes and nothing else. I missed his front side but his back side more than makes up for it. His shoulders look wide and strong. And his ass fills out those shorts to perfection.

But the best part is his calves. I never knew calves could be sexy before. How wrong I was.

Christmas has come early for this girl! Time to get to work.

I dig around in my closet for a pair of cut off shorts that are nearly indecent. I put them on and twirl around in front of my mirror. My legs are pale white. Tanning and being a redhead do not go together.

No worries. I'll give my new neighbor something else to focus on. I pick out a Smuggler's Hideaway tank top with the words *I believe in mermaids* on it.

Time to fluff up my hair and do my make-up. Once I'm finished, I return to the front window to make certain my sexy cop neighbor is home before putting my plan into effect. I notice him running toward his garage from the other side of the street.

I wait ten minutes before enacting the next step of my plan to seduce my sexy cop neighbor. I dig through my garage until I find the lawnmower hidden behind some gym equipment, I bought but never used.

Usually, I pay the kid down the street a few bucks to mow my lawn twice a month but not this month. There's no way my new neighbor can resist a woman mowing her lawn in this outfit.

After thirty minutes of mowing the front lawn, I'm beginning to think I'm wrong. I'm hot and sweaty but thus far my sexy neighbor has not made an appearance.

Does he not hear me out here working?

I want to give up, but I might as well finish the lawn as long as I'm out here. I do one more row and when I come around the corner, there he is. Standing on his front porch with his arms crossed over his chest. Too bad he's got a shirt on now. I'd love to examine those muscles up close and personal.

He marches off his porch and across the lawn toward me. This plan is working better than I expected. I notice his mouth is moving but I can't hear him.

"What?"

When I still can't hear him, I switch off the lawn mower.

"Hi." I smile at him. "You must be Lucas."

The sight of him up close is positively drool-worthy. My new neighbor is the definition of tall, dark, and handsome. He has dark brown eyes, the color of a stout beer. I do love a good stout. And dark brown hair I'd love to pull on while his mouth explores my body. He can give me beard rash as much as he wants. I'm down for it.

And the best part? He's tall. Several inches taller than me. At five-foot-nine, it's not easy to find men who are taller than me.

"How do you know my name?"

"Welcome to Smuggler's Hideaway," I say instead of explaining how there are no secrets in a small town on a small island. He'll learn all about our nosy ways soon enough. "I'm Chloe."

I don't offer him a hand. The first time we touch won't be when I'm all sweaty. Although, I do hope we touch when we're both hot and sweaty. Something to look forward to.

"Chloe." He grunts. "What are you doing?"

My smile falters at his angry question but I muster on. "What do you think? I'm mowing my lawn."

"At eight in the morning on a Sunday."

My nose wrinkles. I didn't realize it was so early. Usually, I'm a night owl but I didn't sleep well last night. I had a nightmare and couldn't get back to sleep. Stupid childhood memories.

"The early bird gets the worm," I quip since I have no idea why he's bringing up the time. I don't know what the problem is. He was up earlier than me to go for a run.

"The early bird gets a citation from the police for noise pollution."

Is he serious?

"Since when is mowing the lawn considered noise pollution?"

"The city ordinance clearly indicates any noisy activities should not be conducted before 10 a.m. on a Sunday."

"What did you do? Memorize all the city ordinances?"

"I'm a police officer. It's my job to know the rules."

I waggle my eyebrows. "All the better to break them."

He scowls. "I enforce the law, not break it."

Someone's a fuddy duddy. But I bet I can get him to loosen up.

"I'm done mowing now anyway."

"Good." He glances at the lawnmower and scowls. "Are you wearing flip-flops?"

I lift up my foot to show off my sandals. "You like them? They have little seals on them. Aren't they cute?"

"What they are is dangerous. You shouldn't be wearing flip-flops when you're mowing. You could chop a toe off."

"Ew. No thanks. I wouldn't want to ruin my pedicure."

He doesn't need to worry about me mowing again. There's a reason why I hire the neighbor kid to do it. It's hot and sweaty work. There's only one time I enjoy getting sweaty. Hint. It's not when I'm pushing a lawnmower.

A drop of sweat falls down my forehead and I lift the bottom of my tank top to wipe it away.

He clears his throat. What's his problem now? His eyes are filled with heat as he stares at the skin exposed above the waist of my shirt. Oh, yeah. Someone's interested. I decide to test my theory.

"I'm going to go have a shower," I say. "I'm all hot and sweaty."

His eyes flare but he coughs before retreating toward his house. "Enjoy your shower."

Does he want me to chase him? Game on, Officer Lucas. Game on.

While I shower, I plot how I'm going to get my sexy new neighbor to notice me. This week is going to be fun.

On Tuesday, I spend an hour pumping up the tires on my bike until I'm afraid they're going to explode. Lucas doesn't show.

On Thursday, I wash my car. I go all out with a revealing top, tiny shorts, and end up wet and covered in soap suds. No Lucas.

On Saturday, I strut around my lawn watering my flowers while wearing the shortest skirt I own. Still no sign of Lucas.

On Sunday, I decide it's time to pull out the big guns. Go big or go home is my motto.

I dig through my closet for a raincoat. I undress before donning it. I add a pair of strappy high heels to my ensemble. The final touch? An empty dish bowl for the 'butter' I'm going to 'borrow' from my sexy neighbor.

Is this move cliché? Yes. Does it work? I'm betting on it.

I check my look in the mirror and nod in approval. "You got this, Chloe girl. You got this."

I march next door to Lucas's place. I don't give myself a chance to chicken out before I ring the bell.

The door flies open and a little girl answers. "Hello."

I check the house number. Yep. I'm at the right place. I didn't accidentally end up at Mrs. Agatha's house. Lucas lives here. Or, at least, he did last week.

"Natalia!" Lucas hollers from somewhere in the house. "Don't answer the door."

This is definitely the correct house but why is Lucas hollering at this little girl? No one mentioned he had a child.

Is he married? Hold on, Chloe. Don't get ahead of yourself. Maybe he's babysitting for a friend.

"Too late!" the girl shouts before smiling at me. "I'm Natalia. Who are you?"

"I'm Chloe. I live next door. What are you doing here?"

She giggles. "You're silly. I live here of course."

"You live here?"

"Why are you wearing a raincoat? It's not raining."

Because I came over here naked to seduce the man I now fear is your dad? Nope. Not the words I'll ever speak to a small child. Not in this lifetime.

"Is Lucas your dad?" I ask instead.

An arm wraps around her waist and she disappears from view as Lucas shoves her behind him. "I told you not to answer the door."

"Dad," she whines. "What do you think is going to happen? I thought we moved to this Podunk town because it's safe and boring."

My jaw drops open. Dad? Lucas is a dad? Where's her mom? Has he been hiding her, too? I shake my head and force those thoughts away.

It doesn't matter. Lucas is officially off the menu. I don't get involved with men with children. Chloe and children is equal to oil and water. Incompatible.

Instead, I take issue with Natalia's statement. "Excuse me, but Smuggler's Rest is not a Podunk town. It just so happens to be the coolest town on the coolest island on the East Coast."

Natalia peeks around her dad to roll her eyes at me. "Adults always say things are cool even when it's not true."

"Oh yeah?" I raise an eyebrow. "Have you been to *Mermaid Mystical Gardens* yet? Or what about the boardwalk? Have you tried a muffin at *Pirates Pastries?*"

"What's *Mermaid Mystical Gardens?*"

"The coolest amusement park in the world."

She giggles. "You say cool a lot."

I shrug. "What can I say? I'm a cool person."

Lucas clears his throat. "Is there something we can help you with?" He rakes his gaze over my raincoat and I feel my cheeks heat.

Damn. I forgot I was standing here naked for a minute.

"I was going to ask to borrow some butter from you to bake a cake but now I'm craving a muffin from *Pirates Pastries*. I'll catch you later." I wave as I back away. "Nice meeting you, Natalia."

As soon as I'm off his porch, I motor over to my house as quick as I can in these shoes. When I'm home, I put on some clothes before jumping on my bike. I don't know where I'm going but I want to be far, far away from Lucas and his daughter.

Humiliation, my old friend, has come for a visit but I'm not answering the door.

Chapter 4

Hazing – when the new kid gets teased by the other kids. May involve a grumpy seal.

LUCAS

I idle the truck at the curb in front of the park. "You sure you're going to be okay?"

I signed Natalia up for a sports camp for the rest of the summer. I don't want her home alone all day during the school break. Plus, this will be a great way for her to make some friends on the island.

She huffs. "I'm twelve, Dad. I'm not a baby."

"You have your lunch?"

She holds up her packed lunch.

"And you know how to get home when camp is finished?"

She rolls her eyes. "There are these things called phones. They're pretty handy. I can look up an address and directions on one."

I didn't want to get her a smartphone. She's too young for one. I want her to play outside and meet friends. Not spend the day staring at a screen. But my ex gave her an iPhone as a gift.

I refuse to be the bad guy who doesn't allow her to receive gifts from her mom.

I ruffle her hair. "Smart alec."

"Any more questions? Or can I join the other kids?"

"Get out of here."

"Bye, Dad!"

She jumps out of the truck – I'm not allowed to help her out anymore – and rushes toward the other kids waiting in front of the sports park. She doesn't know any of them but she doesn't hesitate. That's my girl.

A car honks behind me and I drive away. Natalia doesn't bother to glance in my direction. I don't know how I'm going to survive her teenage years. Her pre-teen years are brutal enough.

I arrive at the police station in Smuggler's Rest less than five minutes later. Although there are two smaller towns on the island – Pirate's Perch and Rogue's Landing – Smuggler's Rest is the only town with a police station on the island of Smuggler's Hideaway.

I grab my bag and make my way into the station. I had a tour of the station when I was here for my interview so I know my way to the locker rooms.

"Hey," I greet the other man in the room when I enter.

"You must be the newbie."

I sigh. Let the hazing begin.

I offer him my hand. "Lucas."

He grins. "Weston."

I know the name. "My new partner."

He nods. "During your training period. We usually do individual patrols on the island." He slams his locker shut. "I'll see you at roll call."

I check the clock and notice I'm behind schedule. Getting a twelve-year-old ready and out of the door during the summer holidays is not easy. Hopefully, she'll make friends today and be more excited about camp tomorrow.

Once I'm changed into my uniform, I make my way to the meeting room for roll call. Weston waves at me and I sit next to him.

"Settle down," the sergeant orders as she enters the room.

I glance around and notice there are less than ten people in the room. At my previous station, there were at least fifty. I hope this job isn't going to be boring.

"First order of business is our new officer. Lucas Fellows." She points to me and I nod. "He's coming from the big city of Baltimore so make sure to give him a Smuggler's Hideaway welcome."

Great. The sergeant basically just told everyone to go ahead and haze the new kid. I hope I at least don't end up bald with whatever they have planned. Natalia would never let me hear the end of it.

Once the briefing is finished and we've collected our weapons, Weston leads me to the parking lot full of police cars.

"Nice vehicle," I say as we settle in.

"Smuggler's Hideaway earns a decent amount of money from tourism. Speaking of which, you want to join me at Mermaid Karaoke tonight?"

"Mermaid Karaoke?" Is this part of the hazing?

He smirks. "It's awesome. The women dress up as mermaids and sing. Most of them can't sing but the outfits." He waggles his eyebrows. "They're worth the price of admission."

"Sorry, I can't. I'm a single dad and I don't have any babysitters yet." I've never been so happy to have a kid before. Mermaid Karaoke? No, thanks.

"I heard you have a kid. A girl?"

"How do you know? Are there no secrets on this island?"

"You're getting the hang of it." We drive out of town toward the beach. "How are you enjoying your house on Treasure Trail?"

"You're not going to pretend not to know everything about my life?"

"Nope."

"Interesting neighbors."

"Chloe or Mrs. Agatha?"

"Chloe. She…"

I cut myself off before I tell him about how she showed up at my house in nothing but a raincoat. There's no reason to embarrass her. Judging by how red her cheeks were when she fled my house, she was embarrassed enough.

I clear my throat. "She was mowing her lawn before eight a.m. on Sunday."

"Chloe was mowing her own lawn?"

"You know Chloe?"

My stomach burns at the thought of Weston and Chloe being more than friends. What the hell? Am I jealous? I don't get jealous of women. Hell, I was married to Holly and I didn't get jealous when she spoke to other men.

I must have indigestion. I can't possibly be jealous of a woman I barely know being with my partner.

"She's friends with my little sister, Sophia. I've known her since she was a snotty-nosed brat."

I bet Chloe was a cute kid with her red hair and light skin. She probably had freckles and wore her hair in pigtails.

"Does your sister still live on the island?" I need to steer the conversation away from Chloe. I don't appreciate the way my body gets riled up upon merely hearing her name.

"She just moved back."

The radio squawks. "Officer Fellows. Come in, Officer Fellows."

"This is Fellows."

"Tourists called in a disturbance on Reef Road."

"On our way."

Weston hits the sirens and I switch on the lights while he makes a U-turn.

"Are all of the street names on Smuggler's Hideaway unusual?"

"One thing you should know." He grins. "There's nothing usual about Smuggler's Hideaway."

We arrive on Reef Road and Weston pulls to a stop in front of a large crowd of people. I frown. "Domestic?"

"We'll see," Weston sings.

Shit. His grin is not a good sign. Is this part of my hazing? Am I being pranked?

There's no sense in complaining or asking questions. I learned when I first joined the police force twelve years ago. Accept the bullshit. Let everyone laugh at you. It'll be over and forgotten soon enough.

When Weston motions me forward in front of him, I know this is part of my hazing. I force my way through the crowd to reach the center of attention.

I skid to a halt when I notice a seal lying in the middle of the road.

"How the hell did you get a seal here to haze me?"

"This isn't a hazing. This is Sammy. Hey, Sammy."

The seal lifts its flipper and waves to Weston. I rub my eyes. I must be seeing things. Because a seal did not just wave to my new partner.

"Sammy is an escapee from Sealife."

"Okay. Let's get in touch with Sealife and get Sammy back home."

"Nah. Sammy's not going anywhere. Except to get off the road."

"How is this not a hazing?" I ask because he can't seriously think I'm going to move a seal. Seals are wild animals. I shouldn't be touching him. Not to mention he probably weighs five hundred pounds.

"Sammy's a Smuggler's Hideaway resident."

I cross my arms over my chest and glare at Weston. I'm done with the riddles. I have enough riddles and confusion at home with my pre-teen daughter. I don't need the confusion in my work life as well.

"Explain."

"Sammy was at Sealife as a pup. They set him free when he was older but he wasn't interested in living life as a wild seal. He came ashore in Smuggler's Hideaway and hasn't left since."

"And what? You let him roam free through the island?"

"Not free. Sammy's not allowed to pretend to be a traffic stop." He wags his finger at the seal. "Are you?"

Sammy covers his face with his flipper. And here I thought I'd seen it all as a police officer in Baltimore. I was wrong.

"How do we get him off the street?"

"There's one sure way." Weston kneels down close to the seal. "Sammy, get off the road before I call the dog catchers. The dog catchers."

Sammy barks before wriggling off of the road. "Bye, Sammy boy."

"Show's over," I tell the crowd. "Nothing more to see here."

A woman rakes her gaze up and down my body. "I disagree." She bites her bottom lip and flutters her eyelashes at me. "I'll be at Mermaid Karaoke tonight."

"Sorry. I have a kid at home."

Weston slaps my back. "You're using your kid as an excuse?"

I shrug. "I'm recently divorced. I'm not interested in a relationship."

"Not even with Chloe?"

My cock twitches at the thought of my neighbor laid out in front of me. Her red hair spread over my pillow. I bet her porcelain skin blushes a pretty pink when she's excited.

I clear my throat. "I'm on a break until my daughter is older."

Weston rubs his hands together. "This is going to be fun."

I ignore him. The same way I'm ignoring my body. My cock might want to discover all there is to know about Chloe. But it's not happening. I don't need a woman now. Especially not a woman who shows up to my house where my daughter is living without any clothes on.

Chapter 5

Natalia – an adorable preteen who's currently in the middle of a breakdown

CHLOE

I slam the door shut behind me and kick off my shoes. My feet are killing me, my back is sore, and I smell of beer. I work in a brewery. It's not unusual to smell faintly of beer. But I smell like a beer factory since a customer threw his beer at me when I cut him off.

I enjoy a nice drink or two at lunch as much as the next person but there's no reason to be smashed at two in the afternoon. Unless it's the Moonshine and Merriment Festival and you've been hitting the Mermaid Moonshine all morning while watching pirates fight each other.

But the festival isn't for a few more weeks. So, Mr. Drunk At Two had no excuse. And there's never an excuse to waste beer by throwing it.

After I shower and wash my hair, I put on a pair of comfy shorts and a t-shirt. There's no sense in getting dressed up since I'm not going out again.

I make myself a sandwich and plop down on my sofa to eat it. I switch on the television and flip through the channels but nothing interests me.

"How was your day, Switch? What about you, Bait?"

My guppies don't answer. They never do. Probably because they're fish.

I'd love to get a dog to keep me company, but I'm not home enough to care for a dog. I'm usually at the brewery handling the restaurant from eleven in the morning until eleven at night. I can't leave a dog home for twelve hours by himself. I'm lonely. Not cruel.

"Chloe!" Natalia screams before ringing the doorbell.

I rush to the door and fling it open. "What's wrong?"

Lucas's daughter rushes inside. "Shut the door. Shut the door."

"You're freaking me out," I say as I shut the door.

"It's horrible. I'm so embarrassed. I don't know what to do." She flaps her arms up and down.

I grasp her hands. "Tell me what happened. We'll figure this out."

"I got my period!" She bursts into tears and I pull her into my arms.

"Hey. It's okay." I rock her from side to side.

"You don't understand. It's my first period and there was blood on my shorts. Everyone saw."

"Did anyone make fun of you?"

"I'm probably the talk of the summer camp."

I wipe the tears from her eyes. "We'll deal with those kids later. First, I need to know if you're prepared."

"Prepared?" She squeaks.

"Did your dad talk to you about your period? Do you have supplies?"

Her cheeks darken and she glances away. "No."

"What about your mom?"

She scowls. "Mom left us. She sends me presents for my birthday, but otherwise…"

Bitch. How can anyone abandon their daughter? Daughters need love and affection, not presents.

"Let's call your dad."

I grab my phone but she slaps it out of my hand.

"I can't talk about this stuff with my dad."

"Why not?"

I didn't have a dad. I mean I must have had a dad. Otherwise, I wouldn't exist. But I never met him. And my mother never had boyfriends who tried to be a dad to me. Creepy boyfriends, on the other hand? Those she had tons of.

"It's embarrassing. He's a boy."

I kneel in front of her. "Here's the deal, kiddo. I'm your neighbor, not your guardian. I can't take you shopping for what you need without your dad's permission."

Her nose wrinkles. "Oh."

"I'm going to ring my friend Weston now. He's a police officer who works with your dad." Thank goodness for the lack of privacy in this town. I don't have Lucas's phone number but

I know he's working with Weston who happens to be my best friend's brother.

"I won't tell him why I need to speak to your dad, though. That's private."

She nods. "Okay."

"Hey, Weston," I greet when he picks up.

"What's up, wild child?"

I'm thirty and no longer a child but explaining myself to my best friend's brother who witnessed my teenage rebellion years is a waste of time.

"Can I speak to your partner, Lucas?"

"I heard you struck out with him."

"What?" Did Lucas tell Weston what happened with the raincoat incident? What a jerk!

Weston bursts into laughter. "I was guessing but you just confirmed it."

"Whatever. I need to speak to Lucas about his daughter."

"Shit. What's wrong?"

"Nothing's wrong per se. But we need to do some essential shopping Lucas hasn't prepared her for."

"Girl shit?"

"Can you get Lucas for me?"

"He's tied up at the moment."

I groan. "Are you still hazing him?"

Weston chuckles. "It's not my fault he thought he could handle the escaped sheep by himself."

"Can you let him know I took Natalia shopping?"

"I will. Uh oh. Gotta go. Lucas is not the sheep whisperer he thought he was."

I shove my phone in my pocket. "Good news. We're going shopping."

"Um." Natalia bites her bottom lip. "Can we maybe go to another town? I don't want anyone to see me."

I pat her shoulder. "Don't you worry. We're not merely going to another town. We're going on the mainland and getting manicures. The day a woman gets her first period should be celebrated."

"I've never had a manicure before."

"It's your lucky day."

I want to make it a happy day for her. I want her to forget all about the other kids witnessing her panic when she realized she had blood on her shorts.

We arrive back on the island three hours later. When I pull into my driveway, the front door next door opens and Lucas steps out. I guess the sheep crisis is over.

"He looks mad," Natalia mutters.

I don't disagree. He's got his arms crossed over his chest again. If he's trying to be intimidating, he's failing since all I can think about is how I want him to use those arms to lift me up and shove me against the nearest surface.

Stop it, Chloe. No drooling over a man when you're with his daughter. Boring rule but there you have it.

"Come on. I'll walk you over."

I grab the bags from the trunk while Natalia stands next to me biting her bottom lip. "Let's go." I steer her across the lawn to her house.

"When Weston said you were going shopping, I thought you were going to the drugstore. Not buying a new wardrobe."

I follow Natalia and Lucas inside before I respond. "We did go to the drugstore. But we also got our nails done."

He frowns. "Why do you need three big bags from the drugstore?"

"Shall we sit down and I'll explain?"

"Dad," Natalia whines. "Do we have to discuss this?"

I hand her the bags. "Why don't you unpack and I'll talk with your dad?"

"Dad?" He nods and she rushes off.

I wait until the door closes behind her before speaking. "I'm sorry. I did try to reach you. I thought you'd call me back and I could explain why we were gone so long."

"I don't have your number."

"You could have asked Weston for it."

"He claimed he didn't have it either."

I chuckle. "He did? I called him earlier, remember?"

He scratches his beard. "I'm ready for this hazing to end already."

"I don't think he's hazing you. I think he's being Weston."

He growls. "You know Weston well?"

"Yep. We grew up together and he's my best friend's older brother."

He narrows his eyes on me. "And you were involved?"

I rear back. "Involved? Me? With Weston? He's a complete man whore."

"Says the woman who showed up at my house wearing nothing but a raincoat."

My cheeks warm but I ignore them. "I had shoes on, too."

Silence falls and I rush to fill it. I'm not good with silence. It brings back too many memories.

"Anyway, as you must have figured out, Natalia got her period for the first time today. She didn't seem prepared at all."

He scowls. "Holly, my ex, wasn't much of a mother."

I figured as much. "Natalia was pretty embarrassed the other kids knew what happened, but I think she's okay now. A pretty manicure can cure a lot of problems."

"Speaking of which." He reaches for his wallet.

I wave him away. "Don't worry about it. I had a two-for-one coupon."

"And the other stuff? Her supplies?"

He shoves a fifty-dollar bill in my hand and I accept it. "I'll make you a list of the things she needs. And if she has any questions, I'm next door. I gave her my phone number if she wants to talk."

"Thank you."

"No need to thank me. I know how it feels not to have—" I cut myself off before I confess to all of my mommy issues.

Lucas steps closer to crowd me. "Not to have what?"

"Never mind. We're discussing Natalia. Not me."

I inch backward toward the door. He shackles my wrist to stop me. Heat shoots from his hand to my skin. It feels comfortable and exciting at the same time. I bite my tongue before I gasp. Lucas doesn't want me. There's no reason for me to embarrass myself by letting him know how much I want him.

"Thank you. I mean it." He squeezes my wrist before releasing me and stepping back.

I immediately miss the feel of him touching me. I want his arms surrounding me, keeping me safe and warm.

I shake my head. This is not me. I don't need a man to keep me safe and warm. I'm Chloe. I can do it all on my own.

"Y-y-ou're welcome," I stutter before fleeing his house.

Chapter 6

Ex-wife – the reason the 'ignore call' option was invented

LUCAS

"Did everything work out okay yesterday with Natalia?" Weston asks once we're in our vehicle cruising toward the boardwalk.

I rub a hand over my beard as I consider how things would have gone had I been the one to handle things. I'm not prepared for my little girl to become a woman. Menstruation? Puberty? Nope. Not even close to being ready.

"If the other kids give her a hard time about getting her period, let me know. I'll talk to their parents."

"Thanks, man."

He glances over at me. "Did your wife not prepare your daughter?"

"My ex," I growl, "did not enjoy being a mother."

"Good thing Chloe was there to handle everything."

At the mention of Chloe, the memory of how it felt to touch my beautiful neighbor surfaces. It was electrifying. I've never experienced anything remotely similar before. I long to touch the rest of her body to discover how electrifying things can get.

But it's not meant to be. My focus needs to be on my daughter. Especially now.

I lift an eyebrow. "I thought Chloe was a wild child I should steer clear of."

"There's no need to worry. Chloe would never date a man with a kid anyway."

I scowl. "What do you mean? She's great with Natalia."

And she is. Not only did she help my daughter through her crisis, she turned the situation into a celebration. In addition to the manicure, Chloe bought Natalia a bracelet as a present. Not an expensive bracelet like Holly would have bought. But a cute charm bracelet with charms of a mermaid, seal, and surfboard.

"Shit. Of course. Me and my big mouth."

"Now, I'm curious. You can't leave me hanging."

"Sorry. It's her story to tell."

I frown. Did something bad happen to Chloe? I did wonder if there was a story when she cut herself off yesterday. But I didn't want to pry. She's entitled to her secrets.

"I thought there weren't any secrets on the island," I push because my curiosity is piqued. I can't allow myself to have my neighbor but I can learn everything there is about her instead.

"And I thought you'd understand a person's need for privacy. You've avoided all questions about your wife."

"Ex-wife."

The idea of Holly being my wife makes me sick to my stomach. I made *the* classic mistake of marrying her when she got pregnant. I thought she wanted to be a family. What she wanted was a sugar daddy. Why she thought me being a police officer was her ticket to the lazy life is beyond me.

The woman I thought I fell in love with while dating was not the woman I married. Not by a long shot.

"When did you—"

His question is cut off when my phone rings. I glance at the display and grunt. "Speak of the devil."

"The ex?"

I nod before answering my phone. "What do you want?"

Weston parks on the street and motions to the bakery before climbing out of the car.

"I'll have a coffee." He gives me a thumbs-up before strolling away.

"Who are you talking to?" Holly asks. "Is it another woman? Have you replaced me already?"

I don't dignify her questions with an answer and repeat my question. "What do you want?"

"Is that any way to greet your wife?" Holly's voice is no longer accusatory. It's sugary sweet instead. It's the voice she uses when she wants something. I no longer care what she wants.

"You're not my wife anymore. We're divorced since you abandoned us."

She sighs. "I didn't abandon you."

"What do you call it when you pack up all your shit and move out?"

"I made a mistake."

"Only one?"

"Be nice, Luke."

I hate it when she calls me Luke and she knows it. My name is Lucas. The same as my father's.

"What do you want?"

"I told you. I made a mistake."

"Let me guess. Your new man isn't putting up with your shit the way I did for a decade?"

I put up with all of Holly's whining and complaining for Natalia's sake. I wanted my daughter to have a mother. I was a fool. Holly was never a mother to Natalia. Not the kind of mother she deserves anyway.

"Edward was the wrong choice. I never should have left you."

"But you did and now we're done."

"Don't hang up."

I pause with my finger on the disconnect button. "Is there an actual reason for this conversation?"

"Yes." She clears her throat. "I want to try again."

I chuckle. "Again? You didn't try the first time."

"Don't lie, Luke. Who stayed up with the baby when you were off working? Who changed her diapers? It wasn't you."

"Nope. It was mostly my mom."

Thank god my parents lived close by. I don't want to imagine what would have happened to Natalia had they not been close.

I'm such an idiot for not ending my relationship with Holly before she abandoned us. But I won't make the same mistake again. Not with Holly and not with any other woman.

"Luke," she whines.

"Holly."

"There's no reason to bring up the past. We need to start with a clean slate."

"Are you fucking kidding me?"

"Language."

I bark out a laugh. "You are fucking kidding me. We aren't starting over. *We* aren't doing a damn thing. We're over. The divorce papers are signed. We're done. I don't know how else to explain it to you."

"You don't have to be rude. I'm asking for a second chance."

"Second?" I snort. "You've had about a million chances to prove you can be the mother Natalia needs. You failed all of them."

"I can be better. And this isn't about Natalia. It's about us."

"Are you deaf? There is no us."

"Watch your tone with me, Luke. I'm being nice. I don't have to be nice."

"Be a brat, a bitch, I don't care. I'm hanging up now."

"Hang up and you'll regret it."

"Clue in, Holly. I already regret the decade I wasted on you."

"Listen up," she hisses. "You will give me another chance or else."

"Or else what? You're going to stop visiting on Natalia's birthday? Christmas? Oh, wait. You haven't seen Natalia in over a year."

"I will sue you."

"Sue me for what? What is it you think I've done? I've provided for my family. I tried for years to get along with you. But you ignored me, ignored our daughter, and did whatever the hell you wanted. What are you going to sue me for?"

"Custody."

My heart stops and my blood turns cold.

"What did you say?" I grumble.

"You heard me. You will give us another chance or I'll sue you for custody. Sole custody."

"No judge will give you custody of a daughter you haven't seen for a year."

She sniffs. "Because you didn't allow me to visit her. You moved across the country without letting me know. It's been devastating for me."

"You bitch," I grit out. "You lying bitch."

"Who says I'm lying?"

"I do."

"It's really about what the judge believes. And is he going to believe you? A man trying to raise a girl? A man who has an erratic work schedule and isn't home when his child needs him? A man who has a dangerous job? Hmmm… who will the judge believe?"

Fuck. Is she right? Are the cards stacked against me? Can she steal Natalia from me?

"You don't want to raise Natalia as a single mom."

"Which is why I want us to try again. We can be a family."

My jaw clenches. A family? I tried to be a family with Holly. Guess what? It's impossible to make a family with a woman who's never around. Who spends all her time avoiding her daughter and husband.

"I am not giving you another chance."

I don't care what I have to do to keep Natalia. I am not exposing my daughter to her mother's toxicity again. It's not an option.

"I guess you'll be hearing from my lawyer then."

I disconnect the call and throw my phone on the dash.

FUCK!

Chapter 7

Coffee – an excuse to spend some time with your friends. And there are cookies, too.

CHLOE

I climb the stairs from the bar and restaurant at *Five Fathoms* to the offices where Sophia, Nova, and Maya are working. I can't help the smile from spreading across my face. Sophia's home. I missed my best friend.

I peek my head into the office. "I'm going for a coffee run to *Pirates Pastries*. Who wants what?"

Sophia groans. "I need a coffee."

Maya giggles. "No sleep with Flynn last night?"

My happiness dims. Sophia is with the man she's wanted since for-freaking-ever. But he's also the man who drove her away from Smuggler's Hideaway *and* the man who's keeping her a secret. I'm not impressed.

"Tell us more. Tell us more," Nova chants.

"Yeah, Sophia, tell us all about how Flynn can't wait to shout to the world about how much he wants you."

Sophia scowls at me. "It's complicated. He's my best friend's brother."

I don't understand why Flynn being Weston's best friend is an issue. Weston's a cool guy. I can't count the number of times he looked the other way when we got in trouble in high school. He didn't even arrest us when a sheep ended up in his squad car. Which he shouldn't have. Since we had nothing to do with the entire situation.

Nova jumps to her feet. "No fighting."

I sigh. I don't want to fight with Sophia. She's been my best friend since I saw her get dropped off at kindergarten by her mom. When her mom kissed her and told her she loved her, I knew Sophia was going to be my best friend. I would have done anything to be near a mom who loved her daughter.

"I need coffee. What does everyone want?"

Sophia stands. "I'll go with. I could use a break."

Nova grabs her purse. "I'm in."

"Don't forget me." Maya rushes after us. "I need a shipwreck cookie."

Nova frowns. "I prefer a Blackbeard's revenge cookie."

"Revenge cookie? Who do we need to prank?"

I have a pretty good idea who Nova's annoyed with but I can't resist teasing her. Nova is all sunshine and smiles and 'life is wonderful' unless we're talking about a certain someone.

We exit the rear door and Paisley hurries toward us. "What are you doing here?"

She purses her lips. "Am I not allowed to join my friends for coffee?"

"Sorry." I immediately backpedal. "I just figured you were busy concocting some special recipe for a super secret beer you're working on."

She grins. "I am working on a special recipe but I have time for a coffee break."

"You're certain it won't explode while you're away?"

"My experiments don't always explode."

I giggle. "But they do sometimes."

"High school experiments don't count."

I lock arms with Sophia and we head toward *Pirates Pastries*. The bakery isn't far. Nothing's far in the town of Smuggler's Rest. I love it. I love knowing all the locals. I love not wasting time on commuting back and forth to work. And I seriously love how close my friends are.

Although, since we're all busy with the brewery, we don't have as much time to socialize as we used to. If it were up to me, we'd live in a big house together and spend all of our free time hanging out. Maybe then I wouldn't be lonely.

I push thoughts of loneliness away. I have everything I want with me now. There's no need to be melancholy at the moment.

"Uh oh. Do I need to phone the police the girls are back in town?" The owner, Parker, asks when we enter the bakery.

Maya snorts. "Chloe would love you to phone the police. A particular police officer, in fact."

I elbow her. "We haven't done anything wrong."

"Yet," Parker mutters before raising her voice. "What can I get you?"

We order several coffees and more cookies than we need considering it's only an hour before lunch. But no one can tell me not to eat cookies ever again.

Paisley glances around the bakery as we wait for our order. "It's extremely quiet."

Huh. She's not wrong. We're the only customers in the place. Usually, it's packed in here. Although, now that I'm thinking about it, I remember it's been quiet the past few times I've been in.

"I don't think the bakery's doing well," Sophia whispers.

I don't understand. Parker bakes the best cookies on the island. She should be raking in the dough. Pun intended.

"Your order is ready," Parker announces before we can discuss the issue further.

We grab our coffees and cookies and wave goodbye. We exit the bakery and begin to make our way back to the brewery.

"Chloe!" Natalia shouts from across the street where she's walking with her dad. I wave at her since my mouth is full of cookies, and Lucas scowls at me.

What's his problem? I thought since I helped Natalia out with her first period, he'd lighten up. I guess not. Too bad his scowl is sexy as hell.

"Who is she?" Sophia asks.

"It's her neighbor's daughter," Nova says.

Sophia gasps. "The neighbor, as in the sexy cop next door, who won't give her the time of day?"

I flick my hair over my shoulder as if I don't care about Lucas. "I don't want Lucas to give me the time of day."

Sophia rolls her eyes. "Tell me more."

Paisley clears her throat. "I can summarize for you. Chloe showed up at Lucas's house naked."

"It was an accident." It wasn't but I'm willing to die on this hill.

Paisley ignores me and continues, "Lucas wasn't interested and his daughter, Natalia, asked why she was wearing a raincoat when it wasn't raining."

"If the scenario you're explaining had happened, and I'm not saying it did, it was because I didn't know about Natalia. Like I said, it was an accident."

Sophia bursts into laughter. "How do you accidentally show up at your neighbor's house naked?"

"I forgot to put on clothes when I went over to borrow some butter. If it's a crime, arrest me."

Maya snorts. "She wants Lucas to arrest her."

She's not wrong. I've had more than one sexy dream of Lucas, handcuffs, and me naked in bed. I nearly fan myself but considering how closely Sophia's watching me, I shove the rest of my cookie into my mouth instead.

I don't know what's wrong with me. Usually, if a man isn't interested, I move on. But Lucas has me all out of sorts. I blame the heat that exploded between us when we touched. I want to explore it. Find out if we can burn up the flames.

But Lucas has made his view perfectly obvious. He wants nothing to do with me.

Chapter 8

Loneliness – can occur even when surrounded by the four best friends a woman could ask for

CHLOE

My heart squeezes as I watch Sophia and Flynn declare their love for each other in front of the whole island. Don't get me wrong. I'm happy for them. But I also realize this is the beginning of the end. All of my friends will fall in love and then where will I be? Alone. Again.

Just like when Mom would— Nope. I shake those thoughts out of my mind. I am not thinking about Mom today. Or any other day.

I stand. "Who wants some Mermaid Moonshine?"

Today is the Moonshine and Merriment Festival. Thus, Flynn dressing up as a pirate and declaring Sophia his wench. A pirate fight is part of the festival tradition. Although, usually, it's a pretend fight and not a man actually declaring his love to my best friend.

The best part about the festival is Mermaid Moonshine. We love our moonshine on Smuggler's Hideaway but Mermaid

Moonshine is especially beloved. It's Smuggler's Hideaway moonshine mixed with blue curaçao and edible glitter. It makes your tongue turn blue but it's totally worth it.

"I'll go with you," Maya says.

I wave away her offer. "I'm good."

I need a second to myself. A second to let my guard down. A second to not be the happy, crazy friend everyone counts on to lighten the mood. My happiness is a complete act but my friends don't notice. They never do.

The line for drinks is a mile long. Good. I can have more than a minute to myself.

"Chloe!"

I wave at Natalia. My little next door neighbor is sweet and adorable. Too bad her sexy dad has no interest in me.

"Oof," I say when she barrels into me.

"This festival is the best. There were two pirates fighting."

"Guess what?"

"What?"

"I know those two pirates. One is my best friend's boyfriend and the other is her brother."

She gasps. "Wow."

I ruffle her hair. "Don't be impressed. Smuggler's Hideaway is a small place. Soon enough you'll know everyone on the island who's around your age."

She frowns. "I hope they're not all mean."

"Mean? Who's being mean to you?"

She rolls her eyes. "You remind me of Dad. What did she do, Natalia? You should report her, Natalia." She mimics Lucas's deep voice.

"I don't believe in reporting bullies. I believe in getting even."

Her eyes widen. "Getting even? How do you get even?"

"Natalia, Natalia, Natalia. Have you not been introduced to the wonderful world of pranks yet?"

Her nose wrinkles. "Pranks are bad."

I tweak her nose. "Now you sound like your dad."

She shrugs. "I don't want anyone to get hurt. I just want Sheila to be nice to me."

"Sheila? Is Sheila here today?" Natalia may think pranks are bad, but I don't. "A bee in Sheila's brownie will teach her." Not a real bee. A fake bee will do the trick.

Natalia giggles. "You're silly."

She thinks I'm joking. I'm not. I will not allow anyone to be bullied. Bullies are the worst.

"Next!"

"Stuck working today, Sloane?" I ask the bartender from the *Bootlegger* bar when I reach the counter.

"The tips more than make up for working during a festival." She nods to the overflowing tip jar. "What can I get you?"

"Four pints of Mermaid Moonshine and…" I glance down at Natalia. "What do you want?"

"Can I have moonshine?"

"Not yet. A few more years."

Natalia is twelve. She has more than a few years before she can legally drink. Although, the drinking age isn't strictly enforced on the island in the winter months when the cold wind is whipping off the Atlantic and the ocean is too cold to swim in.

"A lemonade, please."

Once I've paid, I hand Natalia her drink before gathering the four pints.

"I can help."

"Your dad will kill me dead if I let you help carry alcohol."

She giggles. "Kill and dead are the same thing."

"Let me rephrase. Your dad will kill me and then resuscitate me so he can kill me again if I let you carry any alcohol."

"You don't believe in zombies, do you?"

I widen my eyes. "Zombies are real. Are you not ready for the apocalypse?"

We weave our way through the crowd and away from the line. "Do you want to sit with me and my friends?"

"Yes!"

I notice Lucas walking toward us in the crowd. It's hard not to. He's several inches taller than everyone else. But he's not some string bean. Not Lucas. His body is packed with muscles from his chest down to his calves.

I didn't know calves could be sexy until Lucas. Now I know the truth. Calves can be sexy. As are thighs, pecs, and any other muscle my sexy neighbor has.

"Go ask your dad if it's okay."

"Do I have to?" she whines.

"I don't make the rules."

"Dad!" Natalia waves him over. He grins at her as his legs eat up the distance between us.

"Natalia, what are you drinking?" he asks when he reaches us.

"It's lemonade. Chloe got it for me."

He reaches into his pocket. "Let me pay you back."

"It's fine."

His gaze meets mine and I'm sucked in by those dark brown eyes. They're mesmerizing. I could get lost in them. Preferably while I stroke his beard or spear my hands through his wavy hair.

I clear my throat. No drooling over your next door neighbor who's made it perfectly obvious what he thinks of you. Not a lot.

"Can Natalia hang out with us for a while?" I ask.

He crosses his arms over his chest and I try to ignore how his biceps flex with the motion. I lose the battle. It's a toss up which is sexier. His calves or his biceps. I'd have to touch them to make a decision.

Which will not be happening, I remind myself. Lucas doesn't want to roll in the hay with me. He's made himself perfectly obvious.

"Actually." He clears his throat. "I need to speak to you."

"Go ahead." My arms are aching from holding the four pints, but I want to hear what he has to say more than I want relief for my arms.

"There you are," Nova says as she walks toward us. Maya and Paisley are following her.

I hold up the drinks. "The line was obnoxious." I nod to Natalia. "This is my neighbor, Natalia. She's going to hang out with us today. Assuming it's okay with her dad."

Lucas clears his throat. "I took the day off to spend it with my daughter."

"We won't steal her away then," I say. "I'll see you soon, Natalia."

"Wait!" Lucas orders before I have a chance to escape. "I do need to speak to you."

I raise my eyebrows. "About what?"

"Dad wants you to marry him because my mom is threatening to sue him for sole custody," Natalia answers.

My jaw drops open. Lucas wants to marry me? The woman who, according to him, is more annoying than itching powder in a jockstrap.

Nova wraps an arm around Natalia's shoulders. "We should let your dad and Chloe be alone to discuss this." She leads her away but Maya and Paisley don't follow. "Come on. Give Chloe some privacy."

Maya sighs. "But it's romantic."

"We'll leave you alone," Paisley says as she drags Maya away.

I face Lucas. "It's possible Natalia has been watching too many movies."

He rubs a hand over his jaw. "Actually."

Chapter 9

Proposal – when you ask your sexy neighbor to marry you to save your daughter

LUCAS

I wasn't planning on discussing my idea of faking a marriage with Chloe at the festival but Natalia let the cat out of the bag. Time to man up.

"Shall we go somewhere private to discuss this?"

Chloe bites her lip as she considers my question. I want to be the one biting her lip. I want to taste her mouth. Inhale her scent. Memorize every inch of her.

"Um, most places are closed for the festival but *Pirates Pastries* is open." She points across the street to a bakery.

I place a hand on her lower back to guide her through the crowd. She shivers and my cock perks up. It knows what it wants and can't understand why I've resisted Chloe this long. Especially since she's made it obvious she's interested.

I nearly lost my battle to resist her the day she cleaned her car. Wet and soapy is a good look on her.

"Hi, Parker!" Chloe greets the woman behind the counter when we enter. "I'm surprised you're open today."

Parker frowns. "I thought it would be a good day to earn some extra income but everyone started drinking at nine a.m. Apparently, muffins and moonshine don't mix."

"It's your lucky day. I have a big order. I need a dozen baked peaches and cream whiskey muffins, a dozen pirate's plunder muffins, and a dozen shipwreck cookies. Oh, and a dozen of Blackbeard's revenge cookies."

Holy shit. She ordered enough muffins and cookies for the entire island. What is she going to do with all that food? There's no way she can eat all of it. She has nowhere to put it.

Parker stares at her. "Are you sure? You'll clean out my supplies."

"Awesome. Then, you can go enjoy the festival." Chloe smiles at her. "Can you wrap everything up for me?"

"I'll grab a box." Parker disappears to the kitchen.

"Do you think she bought it?" Chloe whispers to me.

"Bought what?"

"How we came in here to do this big order?"

Now I understand. She's helping Parker. I squeeze her shoulder. "She's thankful either way."

Her nose wrinkles. "I don't want her to think I pity her. Pity's the worst."

Parker returns before I can ask why her smile dimmed. What happened to Chloe? Why does she fear pity?

This woman intrigues me. She presents herself as this happy go lucky woman but there are layers and layers to her. I want to peel each layer away to discover the real Chloe. I don't think many people know the real Chloe.

"Do you mind if we sit and chat in the corner while you get our order ready?" Chloe asks.

"I'll make you some coffee."

I follow Chloe to the table furthest away. We sit down but I wait until Parker has delivered our coffees to speak. She arrives with our coffee and an assortment of cookies.

"I need to get some cookies out of the oven. I'll be in the back." She winks at me.

I chuckle. "I guess we're not being very discrete."

"Parker's a sweetheart. She knows I don't enjoy having my business spread all over town."

Chloe picks out a cookie. She moans as she eats it. My cock hardens and lengthens as I imagine her moaning while in bed with me. While I explore every inch of her alabaster skin with my hands and mouth. I bet her skin is smooth, but I need to touch her to make sure.

"Don't make me eat all the cookies." She motions to the plate. "I mean, I will. Don't test me."

I grab a cookie. "You eat cookies?"

Her mouth drops open. "What kind of question is that? Of course, I eat cookies. I'm a woman. It's my right and privilege to eat cookies. Preferably chocolate."

Huh. I thought with her slim figure, she starved herself. Holly certainly enjoyed starving herself. It drove me crazy. Whenever we went out to a restaurant, she'd pick at a salad while constantly asking me why I wasn't finished yet.

Speaking of Holly. I clear my throat. "My wife is suing me for sole custody."

Chloe gasps causing her to drop her cookie. "Are you kidding me? The woman who abandoned Natalia and didn't prepare her for her first period wants sole custody? Over my dead body. Is she on the island? I know the police. I bet we can banish her from Smuggler's Hideaway."

Warmth spreads through me at her mama bear display. This is what I want for Natalia. Someone to fight for her. Not someone who uses my daughter as a pawn in her game.

"She's not on the island."

Chloe scowls. "She sent her lawyers? How rude."

"Actually, she hasn't sued me yet."

She motions me to continue with her hand. "There's more to the story. Explain."

"Holly—"

"Was she a cheerleader? Holly sounds like a cheerleader."

"She was," I admit.

"We don't approve of cheerleaders. Nova tried out to be one and the entire cheerleading squad was mean to her. Sure, she accidentally tripped a few of them, but an accident is not an excuse to say she's banned from cheerleading for life."

I can't help smiling. Chloe is a hoot. She's crazy. But she's a hoot.

"Holly, the cheerleader, wants to try again."

"To try what again? To be a decent human being? I think that ship has sailed off the edge of the ocean and sunk in a black hole never to be located again."

She's not wrong.

"Try to be with me. To be a family," I explain.

"Aren't you divorced?"

"Holly left us two years ago. I filed for divorce immediately."

"Maybe she's bluffing. She was probably mad you wouldn't give her another chance – I know I would be – and she threatened you to try and get what she wants."

Chloe would be mad if I didn't give her a chance? Is she mad at me now? I did ignore all of her not so subtle overtures at seducing me. Ignored but definitely noticed.

"I can't chance it," I admit. "I can't chance losing my little girl."

"I get it. I wouldn't chance losing Natalia either. She's precious."

Warmth fills me at her words. Holly never thought Natalia was precious and she's the woman who birthed her.

"Which is why I think we should get married."

She pretends to clean out her ear. "I think I'm hearing things. I might be hallucinating. Probably since the moment Natalia said you wanted to marry me. Maybe her announcement caused me to have a stroke. I've heard you can have super realistic dreams while you're in a coma."

I clasp her hands and electricity sparks between us. My cock presses against my zipper. It's hard and heavy and ready to sink into Chloe. I breathe through my nose until the sharp edge of desire softens a bit.

It's not gone. It's never gone when I'm around this woman.

"You're not in a coma."

"Are you sure? Real life Lucas doesn't touch real life Chloe. He prefers to reject her."

The pain in her voice whips at me and slices me open. I never meant to cause her any pain. I don't want her to hurt. But my attention needs to be on Natalia. I can't lose her. I can't let my ex get her greedy hands on her.

"I'm not rejecting you now. I'm asking you to marry me."

She snorts. "As some sort of marriage of convenience."

"I know this isn't ideal. You probably want a man who matches you to marry you." I swallow a growl at the idea of her marrying any man other than me. "But I need help and you've been kind to Natalia. She knows you. She trusts you."

"Because I'm pretty awesome."

Her eyes flare and I realize I'm stroking her wrist with my thumbs. I pull my hands away. I don't want Chloe to get the wrong idea. This marriage will be in name only.

"This wouldn't be a real marriage. But you would need to move into my house to convince a judge it is real. I can't think of any other way to keep custody of Natalia."

Her nose wrinkles. "I prefer to stay in my own house, but I understand why I'd need to live with you."

"There are plenty of bedrooms. We wouldn't have to share."

"I know. I love your house."

She does? I bet she'd look damn fine cooking in the kitchen while Natalia and I set the table. I force those thoughts away. I wasn't lying. My marriage to Chloe wouldn't be real.

I blow out a breath. "What do you say? Will you marry me?"

"For Natalia's sake?"

I nod. "For Natalia's sake."

"Of course, I will. I'd do anything for that little girl."

"You were going to say yes the whole time?"

She picks up another cookie. "Duh. Your bitch of an ex isn't getting her hands on Natalia." She growls as she tears into her cookie.

Chloe is a true mamma bear. I knew she was the correct choice to ask to marry me in this charade. She'll do what's necessary to keep Natalia safe.

"Thank you."

She waves away my gratitude. "I'm not doing it for you. I'm doing it for Natalia."

Damn. She's perfect. Keeping this marriage strictly professional is going to be the most difficult thing I've ever done.

Especially since I'm having a hard time remembering why our relationship has to remain professional in the first place.

Chapter 10

Warning – when four best friends corner you in a room. May involve the loss of eyebrows if unheeded.

LUCAS

I open the door to Chloe's house and—

"Surprise!"

I rear back at the loud cheers. Chloe rushes to me – a strained smile on her face.

"I thought we were meeting to discuss the wedding arrangements."

"These bozos decided we needed a party to celebrate our engagement." She grasps my hand to pull me outside. She shuts the door behind us and leans against it. "I'm sorry. I didn't know they planned this."

I rub a hand down my beard. "Don't your friends know the marriage isn't real?"

She blows out a breath. "They do. But nothing can stop a Smuggler from throwing a party."

"We're having a wedding and a reception in a week."

She sighs. "I know. It—"

"How would it look at the wedding if you don't know your bride's best friends?" a woman asks as she walks around the house toward us.

Chloe glares at her. "Did you sneak out the back door to spy on us?"

"It's not spying when the whole purpose of the party is for us to get to know Lucas," she says.

Three women follow her. I recognize them as Chloe's friends from the *Moonshine and Merriment Festival.*

One is wearing glasses and slides them up her nose. "She does have a point. It would be unusual for a groom not to know his bride's four best friends."

Chloe sighs. "Fine. Lucas, these are my friends." She points to the first woman. "This is Sophia." She motions to the woman with the glasses. "And Paisley. The one smiling at you is Nova and the other one hiding behind Nova is Maya."

Maya waves from where she is indeed hiding behind the others. "Hi."

"I'm Lucas Fellows," I greet them. "Chloe's fiancé."

"Can we go inside now?" Chloe asks. "Mrs. Agatha is peeking through her curtains at us. Before you know it, she'll have spread rumors about us having an orgy with Lucas on my front lawn."

Paisley clears her throat. "Did you know orgies originally began in Roman times to honor Bacchus?"

Chloe opens the door. "You can tell us all about it inside."

"Well, that's disappointing," a woman says as we enter. "I thought the future bride and groom were getting a little nookie time."

"Lily," Chloe scolds. "Lucas and I aren't involved as you very well know."

Lily grins. "I can hope, can't I?"

"You are a bad influence." Chloe clears her throat. "Lucas, this is Lily."

I shake her hand. "It's nice to meet you."

Lily rakes her gaze up and down me. "It's very nice to meet you."

"Sweet flower," a man grumbles before placing a possessive arm around her waist and hauling her close. "Stop ogling the boy."

I'm thirty-five. I'm hardly a boy. But I don't contradict the man.

I hold out my hand. "Lucas."

"Jack." He squeezes my hand to the point of pain, but I'm not sure what message he's trying to send.

"Jack and Lily are Sophia and Weston's parents," Chloe explains. "You know Weston, of course."

Weston strolls over to us. "Hey, partner." He claps me on the back. "I'll be your best man."

"I didn't ask you to be my best man."

He grins. "Who else are you going to ask? Sophia's boyfriend?"

"I don't know Sophia's boyfriend."

"Exactly." He winks. "I'm proud to accept the role of your best man."

"I still didn't ask you."

"I already ordered my tux."

I scratch my beard. "Your tux?"

He motions to Chloe. "This one wants a formal wedding. Didn't she tell you?"

Chloe glares at him. "We're getting married on the beach."

"But the ladies love it when I wear a tux." He waggles his eyebrows.

"Man whore," she mutters under her breath.

I don't contradict her since she's not wrong. "Maybe I don't want a best man," I say instead.

"Chloe has four maids of honor. You need at least one person on your side of the aisle."

"What about your family?" Lily asks. "Perhaps your brother could stand with you."

"I'm an only child." It's a good thing, too. Since I don't plan on telling my parents about the wedding. Hopefully, Chloe and I will be happily divorced before they realize Holly's trying to steal their grandchild.

I glance down at Chloe. My future wife. The idea of divorcing her makes my stomach cramp and my cock protest. But it's for the best. I need to concentrate on my daughter. Natalia needs all of my attention now.

"This wedding is a charade," I remind Weston. Chloe jerks at my words, but when I look at her, she gives me a thumbs up. "I don't need anyone on my side of the aisle."

"Flynn can be on your side," she suggests.

"Who's Flynn?"

"Sophia's boyfriend and Weston's best friend."

"Come on, I'll introduce you." Weston tries to steer me away but I hold my ground. Chloe was ambushed by this party as much as I was. I'm not going to abandon her if she's uncomfortable.

I lift an eyebrow at her. She shoos me away. "Go on. I'm fine."

The strain around her eyes tells a different story, but I don't know her well enough to understand why she's stressed. And I can't ask her in front of all her friends. I don't know much about her but I know she values her privacy.

I look forward to figuring out why. I force those thoughts away. I'm not getting to know Chloe better. This is a business arrangement and nothing more.

"This is Flynn," Weston introduces and I force my thoughts back to the moment.

"Nice to finally meet you. Sophia hasn't stopped talking about you in days. A bit annoying when your woman is obsessed with another man. I had to punish her." He winks.

Weston groans. "No talking about my sister and sex."

"I have to listen to your sexual experiences."

Weston smirks. "I prefer the word escapades."

"Hey, pirate men." Sophia sidles up to her man. "Can we steal Lucas for a minute?"

Weston frowns at her. "No shaving his eyebrows. Or painting his fingernails. Or cutting his hair."

Sophia rolls her eyes. "I wouldn't do any of those things."

"Do I need to remind you of the time you shaved my legs and painted my toenails?"

"Do I need to remind you of why I did those things?"

Flynn chuckles before kissing Sophia's forehead. "Go on."

She shackles my wrist and tries to drag me away. I plant my feet. I'm not fired up to spend any time with someone who readily admits to shaving her brother's legs.

Weston elbows me. "Go. They won't hurt you when the sun's up."

I allow her to drag me down the hallway. She shoves me into a room where the rest of Chloe's friends are waiting.

"What's going on?"

"It's not a big deal," Nova says with a big smile on her face.

Sophia shuts the door behind her and blocks it. My brow wrinkles.

"What's going on?"

"This is the part where we warn you that if you hurt Chloe, we'll come for you," Sophia says.

"I'm not going to hurt Chloe. This is a business arrangement."

"Nevertheless. You will not toy with her feelings," Paisley says.

"She's been hurt enough," Nova adds.

"She's not as strong as she portrays herself to be," Maya whispers.

"What happened to her?" I ask.

Sophia shakes her head. "We're not saying anything happened to her. We're just warning you to be gentle with her."

I scowl. "I'm not an asshole."

"Sophia Milton," Chloe yells from the hallway. "Open the door this instant or I'll tell Flynn about the time you told his high school girlfriend he had herpes."

Sophia yanks the door open. "You wouldn't!"

Chloe crosses her arms over her chest. "Try me."

"Some best friend you are."

Chloe motions to the women in the room. "I'm not the best friend who's warning my fiancé off."

"But—"

"Nope. I'm not listening to whatever reasoning you've come up with in your crazy mind."

"Ahem." Nova clears her throat. "We all agreed."

Chloe rolls her eyes. "Please. I know Sophia roped all of you into doing this." She motions to the hallway. "Off you go."

Sophia stomps away. Paisley and Nova follow her. Maya trails behind. "Sorry," she mutters as she passes me.

"I apologize on their behalf," Chloe says once we're alone.

"No need to apologize. They care about you."

She rolls her eyes. "They have a funny way of showing it. Trying to convince you not to marry me."

I start to correct her but stop myself. Chloe won't appreciate knowing her friends are worried about her. She prides herself on being a strong woman.

There's obviously more to her than the confident woman she portrays to the world. Consider me intrigued.

I want to reach for her. To pull her into my arms and comfort her. But I fist my hands to stop myself.

This is a business arrangement.

Nothing more.

Nothing less.

Chapter 11

Friends – people who support you despite thinking your actions are cray-cray

CHLOE

I stare at myself in the mirror. I can't believe I'm wearing a wedding dress. Not one of those lavish gowns with a long train – I would never wear one of those – but a wedding gown nonetheless. Me in a wedding gown?

I wasn't one of those girls who dreamed of having a fairytale wedding. You have to get married to have a wedding, and I never thought I'd get married. After all, what man will accept a woman who doesn't want to have children?

"I can understand why you're marrying Lucas, but I don't understand why you're having a big wedding," Paisley says and brings me out of my reverie.

Sophia scowls. "I don't understand why she's marrying Lucas."

Maya sighs. "I think it's romantic."

Sophia rolls her eyes. "Of course, you do."

Nova crosses her arms over her chest. "What I don't understand is why this wedding is happening at *Hideaway Haven Resort.* You couldn't have this sham marriage somewhere else?"

And miss watching Nova, my sunshiny friend who doesn't let anything get her down, be grumpy? Not on your life. It's my wedding. I deserve a little entertainment. And being a front row witness to Nova losing her mind over the owner of the resort is the best entertainment there is.

"You probably won't even see Hudson." Except I invited him to the wedding. It's my day. I can be devious if I want to.

Nova flips her hair over her shoulder. "I don't know what you're talking about. Hudson has nothing to do with me."

"Can we stop discussing how much you long for Hudson to notice you and get back to the matter at hand?" Sophia motions to me. "She's marrying a man she doesn't love."

It's true. I don't love Lucas. Do I want to strip off all of his clothes and lick every inch of his body? Totally. But love? Nope. I know better than to hop on the love train. It's rickety and the end destination is at the bottom of a cliff. I vote no.

"She can learn to love him."

I wag my finger at Maya. "Don't go thinking I'm the heroine in one of your romance novels. This isn't the first chapter of a great love affair. This is a means to an end. With the end being Lucas's ex-wife, Holly, not getting her dirty paws on Natalia."

"But you'll be living in his house. He won't be able to resist you."

I snort. "Don't worry. Lucas hasn't had any trouble resisting me thus far."

Which hurts. But I get it. His number one priority is his daughter. Natalia's the luckiest girl in the world to have a dad who will do anything to keep her safe and happy. Sure, she doesn't have a mom who loves her but she's better off without her mom. Toxic moms are no fun.

"I understand you're marrying him," Paisley says. "But why the big wedding?"

Because this is my one chance to have a wedding?

"Lucas suggested we have a wedding. He's worried his ex won't believe we're actually married if we get hitched at the courthouse."

"What does it matter what his ex thinks?" Paisley asks.

"Apparently, Holly is quite the story maker. Lucas thinks she'll tell the judge we only got married so he can keep custody of Natalia."

"Spoiler alert. You are."

I glare at Sophia. "What's with you? I thought since you and Flynn are now in love – gag – you'd be all for me getting married."

She clasps my hands. "Getting married to the man you love? Hell yeah. I'd walk over broken glass to be there."

Paisley clears her throat. "No more walking over broken glass."

Sophia sticks her tongue out at her. "I didn't walk on the glass on purpose."

"You wore flip-flops to shop class. What did you think was going to happen?"

"You remind me of Flynn. He's obsessed with my footwear."

"Oh. Does he have a foot fetish? I've never been into foot fetishes before but I imagine everything with Flynn is sexy. The man is sex on two legs." Maya fans her face.

"What would Caleb think of you fanning over another man?" Nova teases.

Caleb is a soldier who went to high school with us. He's also the man Maya's been crushing on since ninth grade.

"What does Caleb have to do with it?" Maya's blush says she wishes Caleb had something to do with it. "He's my pen pal. He's also a gazillion miles away."

"Afghanistan is actually 7,500 miles away. A gazillion miles is not a scientific measurement."

Maya salutes Paisley. "Aye, aye, captain."

"Are we done with the conversation detour now?" Sophia asks but doesn't wait for an answer before she speaks again. "I don't think Chloe should get married."

Nova rubs her hands together. "Are we going to sneak her out the back way? Is she a runaway bride? Should I get a horse ready? Let's blow this popsicle stand."

"My car is parked in front of the cabin," Paisley says.

"I'll pack her stuff." Maya starts picking up my clothes and throwing them on the bed.

"Stop!" I order, and everyone freezes. "I am marrying Lucas. I'm not standing him up."

Maya drops her load of toiletries on the dresser. "Darn. I wanted to watch Lucas chase after you. He's nearly as sexy as Flynn."

I growl. "Lucas *is* sexier than Flynn."

Maya claps. "Yes! I knew you liked him."

"Of course, I like him. I wouldn't marry a man I didn't like."

"But you should marry a man you love. Not a man you like," Sophia pouts.

I clasp Sophia's hands. "I'm happy you've found love." My stomach gurgles with jealousy but I ignore it. I am happy for my best friend. "But I'm not out to find love."

She frowns. "I don't know why not."

"You know exactly why not."

"Having a bitch for a mother doesn't mean you don't deserve love."

My heart pounds in my chest at the reminder of my mother. Fear tries to creep in but I shove it back. There's no need to fear my mother anymore.

"This has nothing to do with my mother."

Sophia snorts. "Liar. Liar. Pants on fire."

"Good thing I'm not wearing pants."

"No. You're wearing a wedding gown to marry a man who doesn't want you. Who wants to use you. You can't expect me to be okay with this." She sniffs and tears well in her eyes.

"Are you pregnant?" Paisley asks Sophia.

Sophia rears back. "What? Why are you asking me?"

"Because you're usually not emotional."

"We can't all be robots the way you are."

Paisley wrinkles her nose and fiddles with her glasses. "I'm not a robot. Realistic androids don't exist yet."

Someone pounds on the door. "Are you ready? The ceremony's about to begin."

"Ready!"

I try to walk to the door but Sophia clings to me and refuses to budge.

"Sophia," I grumble. "Don't ruin my wedding."

This is the only one I'm getting. I'm going to enjoy it no matter how fake it is. I'm walking down the aisle to the sexiest man on the island, eating cake, and dancing the night away and no one can stop me.

"Promise me one thing."

I sigh. "What?"

"Promise me you'll give this a chance. A real chance."

A real chance? This isn't real.

But what if it was? My stomach tingles in anticipation. What if Lucas did love me and want to marry me for me?

I force those fantasies away. Lucas needs me to keep custody of Natalia. This is a business arrangement. Nothing more. Nothing less.

"This marriage isn't real. There isn't anything I need to give a chance to."

"I bet she gets Lucas to fall in love with her. Who's with me?" Nova asks.

Maya raises her hand. "I vote for love."

"I would never bet against Chloe," Paisley says.

Warmth spreads through me. My friends have their doubts about my decision to marry Lucas but they're standing behind me anyway. They'll support me no matter what happens. No matter if he breaks my heart.

Breaks my heart? What a strange thought. Lucas can't break my heart because my heart is not available to him.

The only people my heart has let in are standing in this room with me.

"Please say you're okay with this," I plead with Sophia.

She squeezes my hand. "I support you, my wild child. Whatever you do. I'm right there behind you."

My heart fills with love for my closest friend. If I'm honest, my eyes are feeling a bit itchy as well. I sniff to stop any tears from falling.

"Good. Because we're doing shots and dancing all night long." I march toward the door. "Let's do this."

Despite myself, I'm excited to see my sexy neighbor all dressed up to marry me.

Chapter 12

Speechless – what happens when you watch the woman you're trying to resist walk down the aisle toward you in a wedding dress

LUCAS

"You sure about this?" Weston asks.

"A little late to ask now." I motion to the people gathered in front of us waiting for the wedding ceremony to begin.

We're on a private beach at the *Hideaway Haven Resort.* Rows of chairs are set up in front of where we stand under an arch draped with tulle and decorated with white roses. Along the aisle are lanterns fashioned out of old moonshine bottles. The white chairs are wrapped in pink tulle with images of mermaids on them.

I'm a man but even I can tell this is romantic as hell. I wouldn't have expected this set up to be Chloe's choice but when I told her I wanted to have an actual wedding, this is what she came up with.

I gave in. Of course, I did. Chloe's marrying me to protect my daughter. I'll give her whatever she wants.

"You do realize you're stuck with wild child Chloe now."

I scowl at him. "Chloe's not a wild child."

He barks out a laugh. "She's got you fooled."

Is he serious? Is Chloe not who I think she is? My glance falls on Natalia who's hopping from foot to foot at the end of the aisle waiting for the ceremony to begin.

Weston's wrong. Chloe is a complete sweetheart to my daughter. And when she found out my ex is trying to steal Natalia from me, she switched on Mama Bear mode. She was ready to hunt down Holly and throw her into the ocean.

Chloe's the woman I want around my daughter. Not her own mother. Although, referring to Holly as a mother is a disservice to mothers everywhere.

"Hi, Mom," Weston greets as his mother joins us at the front of the gathering.

"Mrs. Milton."

"It's Lily. You're a member of the family now."

Another unexpected request from Chloe. She wants to be married by her best friend's mom who happens to be my partner's mom. Chloe is full of surprises. I bet she'll surprise me every day of my life.

"Are you ready?" Lily asks.

My pulse increases until my heart is beating against my chest in excitement.

"Yep," I croak. Weston laughs next to me and I kick him, which causes him to laugh harder. Why did I ask him to be my best man again?

I clear my throat. "Yes, I'm ready."

Lily nods to the violinist who begins to play. The violinist was not a request from Chloe. She actually wanted the rock band *Cash & the Sinners* to perform but the owner of the resort, Hudson, nixed the idea.

Natalia begins walking down the aisle. She's the flower girl but instead of throwing rose petals in the air, she blows bubbles.

She reaches me and I haul her into my arms. "Good job, cupcake."

"Love you, Daddy."

I hug her tighter. She doesn't call me daddy very often. These moments are precious. These moments are worth the world. These moments are why Holly will never get her hands on *my* daughter.

She squirms in my arms, and I let her go.

Weston elbows me. "Here comes the bride."

I turn to watch Chloe walk down the aisle. Holy shit. She's the sexiest thing I've ever seen in my life.

She's wearing a form-fitting dress made entirely of lace. It hugs her body from the neckline all the way down to the knees where it flares out slightly in a mermaid style. In case the tight fit isn't sexy enough, the neckline plunges in a deep V in a tantalizing tease.

"You're drooling," Weston whispers.

"Don't be jealous my wife is hot as fuck." Chloe isn't my wife yet but I enjoy the way the words roll off my tongue. *My wife.*

She smiles as she walks toward me and my heart thumps in my chest. I want to pull her into my arms and meld my lips to hers. I want to peel her wedding gown off to reveal her naked body beneath. I've imagined dozens of ways to explore her body while naked in my shower with my cock in my hand.

My cock hardens and lengthens. Shit. I'm wearing dress pants. There's no hiding a hard-on in these.

I force my thoughts away from what I want to do with Chloe to why I'm here. My gaze falls on Natalia who's jumping up and down in excitement. She's why I'm here. She's the reason for this.

Natalia rushes to Chloe. Chloe leans down and whispers something in Natalia's ear before taking her hand. Together they walk toward me.

This is what I want. What I crave. A woman who will stand by my daughter and me when we need it. And it doesn't hurt how sexy Chloe is.

They reach me and I kiss Chloe's cheek.

"Hi, hubby to be."

"Are you sure about this?" I don't want to make a mistake. Not again.

"As sure as I am that mermaids are real."

"But mermaids aren't real."

She giggles. "I'm sure. And mermaids are real."

"Are you two ready?" Lily asks.

Chloe nods to Natalia. "I think you mean three."

"We're ready," Natalia says.

"Welcome smugglers, bootleggers, rumrunners, and mermaids. We are gathered here today to join Lucas and Chloe in matrimony."

Natalia clears her throat.

"And their daughter, Natalia," Lily adds. "Please face each other and join hands."

Natalia shuffles to the side and Chloe faces me with a big smile on her face. She's beautiful on an average day but when she smiles at me? She's beyond beautiful. It's indescribable.

She wiggles her hands at me. "Hold my hands, ya big goof."

I was so busy staring at her, I forgot what we were doing.

"Have you prepared vows?" Lily asks.

I clear my throat. "Chloe, I promise to cherish you always, to honor and sustain you, in sickness and in health, in poverty and in wealth, and to be true to you in all things until death alone shall part us."

"Thanks, big guy."

"You're supposed to say your vows to me now."

"It seemed rude not to thank you for wanting to cherish me forever."

I shake my head.

She squeezes my hands. "Okay, here goes. Lucas, I promise to cherish you always unless you forget to put the toilet seat down, to honor and sustain you as long as you don't complain about my cooking, in sickness and in health but you're on your own with puking because gross, in poverty and in wealth although I have my own money so no need to worry about the poverty thing, and to be true to you in all things until death alone shall part us assuming you die first of course."

"You forgot to say you won't hit him too hard if he snores!" Nova yells.

"Because I'm smacking him if he snores too loud!"

I lean close to whisper in her ear. "I don't snore."

She shivers and I smirk. I love how easily she's affected by me. I bet I could get her to come within minutes of stripping off her clothes. Or maybe with her clothes on?

"Ahem. We're not finished yet," Lily says. "The rings."

"I have them." Natalia digs around in her pockets. "I swear I have them, Dad."

I kneel down in front of her. "It's okay. Take your time. First your right pocket." Her lip trembles when she comes up empty. "Now, your left pocket." A tear escapes her eye when the pocket is empty.

"I'm ruining your wedding!" she wails.

Chloe kneels next to me. "You're not ruining anything. You are perfect in every way. But did you maybe forget you put the rings in the little bag with the bubbles?"

"Yes!" Natalia rushes to the bag on the chair she abandoned. She pulls out two rings. "Here, they are!"

She lays the rings in my hand and I kiss her hair. "Thank you, cupcake."

Chloe holds out her hand and I place her ring on the tip of her finger.

"With this ring, I, Lucas, take you, Chloe, to be no other than yourself. Loving what I know of you and trusting what I do not yet know. I will respect your integrity and have faith in your abiding love for me, through all our years, and in all that life may bring us."

I slide the ring on her finger. Chloe stares down at it.

"Is it okay?" I whisper. The rings are the one thing Chloe didn't help decide on before the wedding. I went to the mainland by myself to buy them.

"It's perfect." Her bottom lip wobbles and I fear she's going to cry. But not my Chloe. She inhales a deep breath. "Thank you."

I lower my voice. No one on the island has to know this wedding isn't real. "You're the one I should be thanking."

She holds out her hand. "Your ring, please."

I give it to her and she places it on my finger.

"With this ring I, Chloe, take you, Lucas, to be no other than yourself. Loving what I know of you, and trusting what I do not yet know, I will respect your integrity and have faith in your abiding love for me, through all our years, and in all that life may bring us."

I'm surprised she doesn't make any jokes the way she did with the vows but she appears dead serious as she slides the ring on my finger.

"By the power vested in me by the island of Smuggler's Hideaway, I now pronounce you husband and wife! You may kiss the bride."

I touch my lips to Chloe's. My intention is a quick kiss but the second I feel her soft lips, I moan. I press my tongue against her seam and demand entrance. She doesn't deny me. She opens her mouth on a soft sigh and I thrust inside.

She tastes of the ocean with a hint of the untamed. I growl as I sink deeper into the kiss. Her hands dig into my shoulders and I haul her close until her chest presses against mine.

I want more. I want her naked pressing against me. I want her begging for my touch. I want her. Period.

A whistle breaks through the haze and I force myself to end the kiss.

Chloe stares up at me with swollen lips. Shit. I wasn't supposed to kiss her. This marriage isn't real.

I don't know how I'm going to resist her now I've tasted her sweet lips. I am in deep trouble.

Chapter 13

First dance – an excuse to touch the man you just married who you can never have

CHLOE

Weston raps his fork against his champagne glass and I groan. He's one of the few people who know this wedding isn't the real deal but the knowledge hasn't stopped him from trying to get me and Lucas to kiss again and again.

"Don't worry," Lucas murmurs against my lips. "Friendly fire will take him down."

"I'll help you bury the body. I have a list of locations prepared for such an occasion."

He barks out a laugh. "Of course, you do."

Since his arm is wrapped around my shoulders, I can feel his body shake with humor. I wish I could feel his body move against mine while we're naked in bed. I bet Lucas is a thoughtful lover. I bet he'd ensure I get off before he comes.

I shiver as excitement rolls through me.

"Are you cold? Do you want my jacket?"

He needs to stop being considerate. At this rate, I'm going to strip him down before the reception is finished. But we've agreed. No sex. No sharing the same bed. No kissing. Although, we kicked the 'no kissing' rule to the curb at the ceremony.

"I'm not cold." It's the height of summer.

"But you shivered."

"I—"

"Stop being a crabapple!" Nova's scream cuts me off.

"Who's yelling at the owner of this resort?" Lucas asks.

"It's Nova." I contemplate explaining the history between Nova and Hudson, but it's Nova's story to tell.

He stands. "Shit. I'll handle this."

I stop him. "Let them be. They've been at loggerheads ever since he came home after his career in the NFL crashed when he was injured."

I suspect before then but Nova refuses to discuss anything having to do with Hudson.

His eyes widen. "I knew I recognized him."

"Don't fangirl on him. He gets grumpier than normal when people remind him of his career."

"I don't fangirl."

"Do you prefer the word fanboy?"

"I am not a fanboy," he grumbles.

Oh boy. I better not tease him anymore because his grumbly voice has my panties dampening with excitement.

"Yeah. Yeah. Save it for someone who believes you."

He tickles my ribs. "I am not a fanboy."

I swat his hands away. "No tickling. I don't want to ruin this dress."

His gaze drops to my chest, and his eyes flare. "Wouldn't want to ruin this dress," he mumbles.

I fist my hands before I slip the spaghetti straps off my shoulders and reveal my naked chest to him. Bad idea, Chloe. Bad idea.

Weston raps his fork against his glass again. I glare at him but he isn't shouting *kiss, kiss*! He's standing.

"I believe it's time for a toast."

I groan. Great. Weston has known me since I was five years old and followed Sophia home like a puppy every day after school. He knows all my secrets. Almost all, I correct. He doesn't know everything about dear old mom. Time for some preventive action.

I raise my glass. "Here's to the bootleggers. Masters of sneaky snips and secret stashes. Thanks for keeping the party alive."

"To the bootleggers!" The crowd cheers.

"Nice try, wild child," Weston says. "As the best man, it's my obligation to make a toast. The more it embarrasses you the better."

Lucas growls before stealing the microphone from him. "You are not embarrassing *my wife* at her wedding reception."

Heat hits my chest and radiates through my body at his words. *My wife.* He doesn't sound as if he's faking it now.

Weston chuckles. "This is fun."

I narrow my eyes at him and he winks back. Lucas slaps him upside his head and he bursts into laughter. *Fun,* he mouths at me.

The singer of the band taps his microphone. "I believe it's time for the couple's first dance."

Lucas offers me his hand. "You ready for this?"

I bite my tongue before I giggle. I'm ready, but I don't think he is.

He leads me toward the dance floor and gathers me in his arms. "What song did you pick?"

"You'll hear."

"Ladies, gentlemen, and mermaids, I present to you Mr. and Mrs. Fellows," the singer announces before beginning to strum his guitar.

Recognition lights in Lucas's eyes. "Wild horses?"

"What can I say? I love the Rolling Stones."

"Another layer to unpeel," he murmurs.

"Layer? What are you talking about?"

He sways to the music. "Nothing, wildcat. Nothing."

Wildcat? Butterflies flutter in my stomach. Did he just give me a nickname? A sweet nickname to match me but isn't rude the way wild child is?

The music ends and I realize my eyes are closed. And I'm clinging to Lucas. So much for keeping this marriage strictly professional.

"Um…" I step away. Lucas holds on for a second longer before releasing me.

An electric guitar plays a mellow rock intro and Sophia, Nova, Maya, and Paisley rush to me. Lucas backs away. "Have fun," he says with a wink.

"I take it all back!" Sophia yells as she and the rest of my friends dance in a circle around me. "I love this marriage!"

I raise an eyebrow at Paisley. "What changed her mind?"

"I believe the fact you appeared ready to copulate with Lucas on the dance floor."

"You were making goo-goo eyes at each other." Maya presses her palms to her heart.

Nova beams at me. "Even Hudson the crabby crab tree can't ruin this moment." My happy friend is never down for long.

But she's wrong. There were no goo-goo eyes. There is no love or affection. This is a business arrangement.

"We've got one more activity for our bride and groom," the singer announces when the song ends. "The cake."

"The cake?" My brow furrows. "I didn't order a cake." I would have but all of the bakers claimed they didn't have time to make one.

"We did!" Sophia squeals as she nudges me toward the corner.

My mouth drops open as I step closer and notice the multi-tiered cake is covered in seashells. There's also a mermaid sitting on top of the cake with a merman. It's the perfect wedding cake for Smuggler's Hideaway.

"It's chocolate stout cake," Paisley explains. "Parker used the Five Fathoms Out of the Blue Stout in the cake batter."

Natalia sprints in our direction and crashes into me. "Come on, Chloe. Dad says I can't have a piece of cake until you cut the cake. I said I could cut it but I'm not allowed to use the cake knife."

I wrap my arm around her shoulders. "I guess I better cut the cake then."

The wedding photographer rushes forward. "Can I get some pictures with you and the cake?"

"Where do you want us, Melody?" I ask as Natalia and I join Lucas at the table holding the cake.

Melody's a few years younger than me. She's not a professional photographer but it's her dream to be one. Since I'm all for women following their dreams, I asked her to be our photographer today.

We pose for shots until Natalia complains. "I'm ready for cake."

I pick up the cake knife. "I guess I better cut this cake then."

Lucas wraps a hand around mine. "I believe *we* better cut this cake."

"Ready?" He nods and we slice one piece of cake before plating it.

"Are we really going to feed each other a piece of cake?" I ask.

"We don't have to do anything you don't want to."

Gah. I could fall in love with this sweet man. He really needs to stop being nice to me. Good thing I have the best idea to help him stop being so sweet.

"I'm good." I give him my back so he won't notice me pick up the entire piece we just cut.

"Me first," I say before whirling around and shoving the entire piece in his face.

"Best wedding picture ever!" Melody shouts.

"Great," Lucas mumbles as he wipes cake out of his eyes. "I was worried you didn't capture the moment."

"Stop fooling around, Dad. I want cake."

"You want cake? I'll give you cake, my little cupcake." Lucas lunges at Natalia and she screeches before running away. He chases after her.

Sophia throws an arm over my shoulders. "Look at you, with your little readymade family."

I slap her arm away. "They're not my family." I lower my voice. "This isn't real, remember?"

"I remember. The question is – do you?"

I can't pull my gaze away from Natalia and Lucas goofing around. I do remember this isn't real. Even though I also wish it were.

But it's not meant to be. I can't be a mother and Lucas doesn't want me.

Today is a show. Tomorrow, we go back to 'normal'.

With a start I realize. I don't want to go back to normal.

Chapter 14

Girl dad – a father who can remove hairpins without causing baldness

LUCAS

"Holy cow," Chloe murmurs when she opens the door to the honeymoon cabin. "Hudson should not have included this in our wedding package. It's too much."

Hudson didn't actually include it. I paid for it. I couldn't help myself. When Chloe suggested we return to my house after the party, she got this sad look on her face. I don't want her to feel sad. I want her to have everything she desires.

"What do you think?"

She throws out her arms and spins around in a circle. "I love it! This cabin is everything."

She smiles at me and warmth fills my chest. Only for Chloe would I fork out the money for this honeymoon cabin. But it's worth it. She's worth it.

"Too bad it's already dark outside. I bet there's a gorgeous view of the ocean from the patio." She opens the patio doors and screeches.

I rush after her. "What's wrong?"

She points to the hot tub. "I didn't bring my swimsuit."

"You can wear your underwear. I don't mind."

"Um." She bites her bottom lip. "I don't have a bra with me." She indicates the front of her dress. "I couldn't exactly wear one with this."

My cock twitches. I've wanted to peel her dress off of her since she walked down the aisle several hours ago. I've been fighting a hard-on for most of the reception.

"You can borrow a t-shirt from me."

Shit. What am I thinking? Chloe in my t-shirt. Wet and see-through from the hot tub. All of her alabaster skin exposed to me. I won't be able to keep this marriage professional in that scenario.

I clench my jaw and fist my hands to stop myself from reaching for her.

She creeps backward away from me. "Maybe we should go home."

"Why?" I know she loves this place.

"You seem angry."

I blow out a breath. I'm not angry. I'm sexually frustrated and fighting to stop myself from attacking her.

We agreed there would be no kissing and no sex during our marriage. I'm trying to keep up my end of the bargain, although I'm finding it difficult to remember why I insisted there would be no sex in the first place.

"Sorry. It's been a long day." Lamer words have never been spoken.

"Are you missing Natalia? Maybe she shouldn't be alone tonight."

"She's not alone. She's with Lily and Jack."

"She's in good hands. Sophia's parents are the best."

"What about your parents? Where are they?"

She shrugs. "I never met my dad and my mom left the island the second after I graduated high school."

"And you don't know where she is now?"

She glances away to stare out at the ocean. Except it's dark and the ocean isn't visible. But I can nearly feel the water. The waves crash against the shore and the air smells of the sea.

"Don't know. Don't care."

She might say she doesn't care but the hurt in her voice says otherwise. I wrap my arms around her waist from behind. She leans into me.

We stand there staring into the dark night for a while. It's calm and peaceful. I don't want to ever move. I could stand here with Chloe this way forever.

Damnit. I'm not supposed to get attached to my wife within hours of marrying her. I squeeze her middle once before dropping my arms and stepping away.

"I'm going to change," Chloe says before fleeing.

I'm going to miss her walking around in that dress. Her wedding dress doesn't hide anything. All of her delicate curves are on display.

But it's better if she changes. I don't know how much longer I can resist temptation.

I decide to change into more comfortable clothes while she's in the bathroom. I open my overnight bag and a box of condoms falls out. Damn, Weston. I throw the condoms in the bottom of my bag and pull out a pair of pajama pants and a t-shirt.

Chloe still hasn't emerged from the bathroom. If she's anything like my ex, it'll be a while. I don't want to go to sleep before she's finished. I'll watch some television while I wait. Except when I plop down on the sofa in the living area, I realize there's no television in here.

"Damnit," Chloe mutters.

I'm on my feet and at the door to the bathroom before I realize I've moved. "Chloe." I knock on the door. "What's wrong?"

"My hair's stuck."

"Can I come in?"

"The door's unlocked."

I nearly swallow my tongue when I walk inside and see what she's wearing now. She has on the smallest pair of pajama shorts in the history of the world. She's paired them with a tank top.

"Can you help?"

I force my gaze away from her breasts and imagining what color her nipples are.

"What happened?"

Chloe's hair is a complete mess. The front tumbles down her face but the back is twisted.

"I can't get the hairpins out."

"Sit down." I motion to the chair in front of the vanity.

"Please be careful. I'm not one of those women who look good without hair."

I disagree. Chloe is gorgeous, with or without hair. She's a classic beauty with her alabaster skin and auburn hair. She could wear a garbage sack and still be gorgeous.

"You're beautiful with or without hair."

She scowls. "I don't want to be beautiful."

"What's wrong with being beautiful?"

"The only thing my mom cared about was being beautiful. The lengths she went to…"

I frown. "What did she do?"

"I don't want to discuss it." She motions to her hair. "Can you help or do I need to phone someone else?"

I growl. No one else is seeing her in her tiny sleep shorts and tank top. "I got this."

I tilt her head forward and begin my search for bobby pins. I remove them one by one until Chloe's hair tumbles down her back and she sighs in relief.

I comb my fingers through her hair to get out the tangles.

Chloe moans. "You're good at this."

I ignore how my cock enjoys the sound of her moan. "I'm a girl dad."

"Natalia is lucky to have you."

I finish untangling her hair and squeeze her shoulders. "I'm sorry you didn't have a dad growing up."

She shrugs. "I had Sophia's dad." She grins. "Jack is the best. He's probably spoiling Natalia rotten now."

"She should be in bed but considering she ate two pieces of cake and drank a crate of coke, she's probably running around the house driving Weston's parents crazy."

She giggles. "You shouldn't have let her drink so much coke."

I offer her my hand to help her stand. I lead her to the living room where we sit on the sofa next to each other, facing each other.

"I didn't let my daughter do anything. Your friends and Weston kept on giving her coke."

She rolls her eyes. "They were trying to ruin our wedding night by making Natalia hyper."

"Weston wasn't trying to ruin our wedding night. He stuffed an extra-large package of condoms in my bag."

Her eyes flare. "He did?"

I feel her pulse spike in her wrist and I realize I'm still holding her hand. I need to pull away. We agreed no sex. Sex will complicate our situation.

My focus should be on Natalia. I won't let her suffer because her mom is a bitch.

With a growl, I manage to pull my hand away and stand. "You can have the bed. I'll sleep on the couch."

Hurt flashes in her eyes but she blinks and it's gone. I have a feeling Chloe doesn't allow anyone to see when she's hurting. And now I'm the cause of her hurt.

I don't want to be an asshole. But this relationship isn't real. Chloe knew it wasn't real going into this marriage.

"The bed is huge. We can be adults and sleep in it together without having sex."

Wrong. I can barely stop myself from ripping her clothes off of her as it is. If we sleep in the same bed, what little resistance I have left will crumble.

She lifts her eyebrows. "Or are you scared?"

I glare at her. "I'm not scared."

"Good. Then, we can share this big bed and you don't have to sleep on the sofa."

"The sofa's fine."

She fists her hands on her hips. "Call me old fashioned but I'm not letting my husband sleep on the sofa the night of our wedding."

Her husband? Those words slam into my heart and fill me with warmth. And fuck it all. I can't deny Chloe what she wants. This does not bode well for me but I'm done fighting for this evening.

"Fine," I grumble before marching to the opposite side of the bed.

Chloe climbs into bed next to me. "FYI. Being grumpy is not a turnoff." She rolls to her side away from me. "Good night, hubby."

I lay with my muscles locked until her breathing evens out and I know she's asleep. She mumbles in her sleep. "Go away, bootlegger. The mermaid is mine."

I bite my tongue to stop myself from laughing out loud and waking her. Even asleep Chloe is cute as hell. Good thing we aren't sleeping in the same bed at home.

Resisting beautiful Chloe is hard enough. Knowing she's cute as hell while she sleeps does not help the situation.

Chapter 15

Cooties – a disease that causes your fake husband to avoid you

CHLOE

My alarm goes off and I slap my hand on the nightstand. At least, I try to slap my hand on the nightstand to end the infernal racket, but I meet air instead. What in the world? Where is my alarm clock?

I force my eyes open and glance around the room. I'm not in my bedroom at home. I'm in the guest bedroom at Lucas's house.

I moved in yesterday after we returned home from our one-night honeymoon where I slept on my side of the bed and Lucas slept on his. There was literally no contact between us.

In fact, when I woke up, Lucas was already dressed and ready to go home. He claimed he couldn't wait to pick up Natalia whereas I'm beginning to think I have cooties.

My alarm is still blaring. I roll out of bed and march to the dresser where I put my phone last night. I switch off the alarm and notice the time. Seven a.m. I should be still snuggled in my bed. But I offered to help Lucas get Natalia to summer camp this morning. As long as I'm living here, I might as well help.

And now I'm awake and need to pee. I don't have an attached bathroom and make my way to the family bathroom in the hallway.

Natalia flies out of her bedroom and dashes into the bathroom before I can get there.

"Hey!" I bang on the door. "I need to pee."

"You snooze, you lose!"

I shuffle from foot to foot as I wait for her to finish but then I hear the shower switch on. Damnit. I can't wait for her to shower. I contemplate running over to my house but I don't think I'll make it.

Desperate times call for desperate measures.

I knock on Lucas's door but don't wait for him to respond. I slap a hand over my eyes and rush inside.

"I need to pee. Can I use your bathroom?"

I try to walk to the bathroom with my eyes covered and end up stubbing my toe on the bed. I drop my hand to check my toe.

"Are you okay?" Lucas asks and I lift my gaze to discover he's shirtless. He's wearing his uniform pants and nothing else. Holy mermaids in the sea! His chest is a work of art. Broad shoulders, more abs than I can count in the morning, and a tribal tattoo covering half of his chest.

"I'm ah...." I babble because my mouth is too busy drooling to figure out how to speak.

He chuckles. "Did you hurt your toe?"

My toe? Oh, yeah. I wiggle it. "It's not broken." My bladder reminds me of why I'm in Lucas's bedroom drooling over him. "Can I use your bathroom? Natalia budged in line."

I rush into the bathroom and do my business as quick as possible. When I return to the bedroom, it's empty. As is the family bathroom.

Crap. I'm not much help with the morning routine if I'm standing in the hallway while Lucas and Natalia are downstairs. I throw on a pair of shorts and a t-shirt before rushing to join them.

"I don't want bran cereal!" Natalia screams. "I'm not an old man."

"Watch your tone, cupcake."

"I can whip up some eggs," I offer.

Natalia feigns gagging. "Eggs are gross."

"What about some toast?"

"I want my normal cereal."

Lucas catches my eye over Natalia and mouths *sorry.* He has nothing to be sorry for. He isn't responsible for his daughter's behavior.

"I have a bunch of cereal in my kitchen back home. Do you want me to go get it?"

Lucas growls. "You're not going to your house because Natalia's being a brat."

"I'm not a brat."

He points to the table. "Then eat your bran cereal."

I snatch my keys from the peg near the front door. I stare at the pegs for a second. There are nametags for each of them.

Dad. Natalia. Chloe. Natalia presented me with the peg when we returned yesterday.

It's the best present I've ever received, which sounds stupid. But all I've ever wanted is to belong to a family. A real family.

This isn't real. This isn't my family. But I'm going to enjoy it while I can. Starting with getting Natalia her cereal.

I open the door but before I can step outside, Lucas snags my keys out of my hand. "I'll go. You don't have any shoes on."

I roll my eyes. "We live on an island. Shoes are optional."

He squeezes my shoulder. "Go make yourself a coffee. I'll be back in a sec."

"The cereal's in the pantry off of the dining area," I holler after him.

"Do you need a lunch for today?" I ask Natalia when I return to the kitchen.

"Oh no. I forgot."

"It's okay. I got this. What do you want?" I open the refrigerator and survey its contents. "Ham and cheese or peanut butter and jelly."

"Ham and cheese with mayonnaise."

I pull out the ingredients and set them on the counter.

Lucas returns with an armful of cereal. "Did you bring the entire pantry?"

He shrugs. "You're not living there anymore. It'll go to waste."

I frown. It wouldn't go to waste. I'll be back in my house as soon as Holly realizes she doesn't have a chance to steal custody of Natalia. How long do custody battles last anyway? I should probably ask someone.

Natalia grabs a box from Lucas. "Thanks, Dad."

Lucas notices me preparing Natalia's lunch and hands me a reusable lunch bag to use. I stuff the sandwich in there along with an apple and a mini chocolate bar.

Once Natalia's lunch is ready, I fix myself a coffee. I've barely had a chance to swallow my first sip when Lucas's phone rings.

As he listens to the conversation, he stands. "We need to go now, kiddo," he says as he places his bowl in the sink. "I have to be at work early."

"But I'm not finished eating," Natalia whines.

"Sorry, cupcake. Duty calls."

"I can drive her to camp," I offer.

"You can drive?" Lucas asks.

"Of course, I can drive. It's awful hard to get all those speeding tickets without driving. I'm fast on my bike but I'm not that fast."

"Smart alec. I've never seen you drive before. You're always on your bike."

I shrug. "What's the sense in driving when I can bike to everywhere in Smuggler's Rest in less than five minutes?"

"You have a car?"

Does he not remember my car wash performance? So much for getting his attention.

I roll my eyes. "No, I was planning on putting Natalia in the basket on my bike." He opens his mouth to protest but I giggle.

"Yes, I have a car. I wouldn't have offered to drive her if I didn't have a car."

"You need to leave in five minutes to drop her off in time."

I salute him. "Aye, aye, captain."

"You haven't had your breakfast yet."

"I can actually drive without eating first. It's a skill I acquired in college when I couldn't stand another peanut butter and jelly sandwich for breakfast."

"You went to college?"

I point to the door. "You need to get to work."

He checks his phone. "Shit. I need to go." He ruffles Natalia's hair. "Have fun today." He kisses my cheek as he passes me. "Thanks for your help this morning."

"Happy to help."

I'm not lying. I am happy to help. I'm happy to pretend to be part of this family for a while. I'll just set my alarm for five minutes earlier tomorrow because I'm not letting a twelve-year-old beat me to the bathroom again.

"Come on, kiddo. Time to go."

I sip on my coffee as she picks up her bowl and rinses it in the sink before placing it in the dishwasher. Well trained kid. She's kind of perfect. I wish she was mine.

"Have fun," I say when we reach the summer camp.

Natalia opens the door but pauses before whirling around to face me. "I want you and Dad to be real."

My breath catches in my throat. "Real?" I croak out.

"I know you married him to keep my mom from getting custody of me, but I like you and I think my dad likes you. Do you like my dad?"

I nod. "Your dad is a great guy."

"But do you like him like him?"

"Natalia, sweetie, it's sweet how you want us to be a real family." A real family? I never thought I'd have a real family. "But whatever happens between your dad and me is between the two of us."

Her nose wrinkles. "Okay."

She jumps out of the car before rushing away. Damn. I hope I didn't hurt her feelings.

The last thing I want to do is hurt Natalia. But I didn't lie. My relationship with her dad is private.

I shake my head. What am I thinking? I don't have a relationship with her dad. Unless you count friendship, which is not what Natalia meant.

Gah. This family stuff is hard.

Chapter 16

Altercation – a noisy argument between two women at a children's rollercoaster. May involve nachos.

LUCAS

"What's going on?" I ask Weston as I enter the station.

"Pay up!" He opens his hand to Officer Ledger who slaps a bill in his hand.

"What did you bet about?"

"You." He smirks. "I bet you didn't use any of the condoms I gave you as a wedding present."

I grasp the back of his uniform shirt before dragging him down the hallway to the locker room and shoving him inside. After making certain we're alone, I shut and lock the door behind me.

Weston grins. "If you want to be alone with me, all you have to do is ask. I do require dinner before I put out, though."

"What the hell are you thinking? You know my marriage to Chloe isn't real."

"Doesn't mean you can't get a little something, something." He waggles his eyebrows.

I wrap my hand around his throat and slam him against a locker. "You will not disrespect my wife. Do you hear me?"

He claws at my hand on his throat. I release him since I shouldn't be choking out my partner. At least not in the police station. "Your wife? The marriage is a sham, remember?"

I don't give the first shit if the marriage is a sham. No one disrespects Chloe on my watch. Least of all a friend from childhood.

Hold on. Weston's known Chloe most of her life. Maybe he can fill in some of the blanks about her history. "What happened with Chloe's mom?"

"What do you mean?"

He knows exactly what I mean. It's why he won't meet my gaze.

"She left the island and Chloe has no contact with her. Something happened."

"Sorry, bro. It's Chloe's story to tell."

Damnit. I can't push him. I don't want Chloe's secrets to be exposed to the whole island. Except I'm not the whole island. I'm her husband. He should—

His radio squawks. "Officer Milton."

"Go ahead."

"There's an altercation at *Mermaid Mystical Gardens*."

"On our way." Weston throws the car keys at me. "You're driving."

"*Mermaid Mystical Gardens* is the amusement park?" I ask as we drive out of town.

"Yep. The entire theme is mermaids."

"What is the obsession with this island and mermaids anyway?" I couldn't believe it when they brought out the cake at my wedding reception and there was a mermaid and merman on the top of it instead of a bride and groom.

"You don't know the legend?"

"It wasn't included in my welcome packet when I moved here."

"Legend has it a mermaid fell in love with a smuggler. There was one little problem, though. The smuggler couldn't live in the sea, and the mermaid couldn't live on the land. But then the mermaid went to a witch and traded her immortality for legs. Meanwhile, another mermaid convinced the smuggler he could live in the sea."

"I sense a tragic ending coming."

"Yep. The mermaid arrived on Smuggler's Hideaway to discover her lover had drowned. She threw herself off the cliffs at *Mermaid Mystical Gardens*."

"And now the entire island is obsessed with mermaids."

"Nah, bro. We're obsessed with bootleggers, moonshine, rumrunners, *and* mermaids. Mermaid Karaoke is the best."

"You're such a player."

He smirks. "And proud of it."

"Some day love is going to knock you over and you won't know what hit you."

"Nah. I don't give women the chance to fall for me. I'm a one-night wonder."

"Your loss," I murmur as I park in front of the entrance to the amusement park.

We get out of the car and make our way to the manager who's waiting for us.

"What's the problem, Oliver?" Weston asks.

"There's a group of women fighting at the *Siren's Spiral* rollercoaster."

"Women?" Weston asks. "The *Siren's Spiral* is meant for children."

"Your sister loves the *Siren's Spiral* rollercoaster," Oliver says.

Weston sighs. "I know the way."

We make our way through the amusement park to the rollercoaster. We pass various rides: *Carol Carousel* – a classic carousel ride with sea creature-shaped seats, *Atlantis Adventure* – a ride through the lost city of Atlantis, *Kraken's Drop* – a drop tower ride with a giant sea monster, *Grotto Rapids* – a water raft ride, and *Triton's Twister* – a spinning teacup ride. The list goes on and on.

We finally reach the *Siren's Spiral*. A crowd is gathered in front of the line for the ride where a shouting match is happening.

"I was here first, bitch!" a blonde woman screeches at a short woman with dark hair and glasses.

"Could you refrain from using adult language in front of the children?" the dark haired woman asks.

"I'll use whatever language I want, bitch!"

"And you weren't first. You left the line."

"I went to the bathroom."

"You were gone fifteen minutes and returned with a tray of nachos."

"What's your point? I'm not standing in line. I'm not some loser."

"You can't budge in line. All of these people have been patiently waiting their turn to ride the rollercoaster."

"Losers."

"Boo!" the crowd roars at the blonde.

"Why are we here?" I ask Weston. "The police aren't needed for this."

He rocks back on his heels as he observes the women shouting at each other. "Just wait. Trust me."

I return my attention to the women.

The dark haired woman frowns. "I am not a loser and I don't appreciate your tone of voice in front of my child."

"Mom, I'm not a child."

The blonde points at the little girl. "Even your kid thinks you're a loser."

"I am not a loser."

"Oh yeah. Would a loser have cheese all over her shirt?" The blonde throws the nachos at the other woman before dumping a soda over her head.

The dark-haired woman removes her glasses. "I tried to be nice," she mumbles before lifting her hand and decking the other woman in the face with her fist.

The blonde falls to the ground screaming, "Assault! She assaulted me."

Weston and I rush forward. I detain the short woman with glasses while Weston helps the blonde to stand.

"I didn't do anything wrong," the blonde screams as she tries to wrench out of his hold.

"I know I shouldn't have punched her," the dark-haired woman says to me. "Would you allow me to phone my husband to mind my child while you arrest me?"

"No need," a man says as he approaches. "You just couldn't help yourself, could you?" He reprimands her but he's smiling. He knew who he married.

"She threw her nachos on me and dumped her orange soda over me. You know how much I hate orange soda."

He barks out a laugh. "Yeah, let's blame it on the orange soda." He kisses her nose before stepping back.

I remove my handcuffs from my utility belt but hesitate when I notice her daughter watching.

"It's okay. My daughter needs to learn there are consequences to your actions."

I place the handcuffs on her wrists. "What kind of rap sheet am I going to uncover when I run your name?"

She winks at me. "None."

There's only one reason she doesn't have any priors. "Damn. You're on the job, aren't you?"

"Special Agent Ashford. Nice to meet you."

"Officer Fellows."

Weston drags the blonde toward us. "Tammi says she's learned her lesson and won't budge in line anymore."

I don't believe Tammi. "We'll have a nice chat down at the police station." Weston nods in agreement.

I lead Agent Ashford toward the exit.

"He can arrest me anytime!" a woman in line hollers as I pass.

"Sorry." I wave my ring finger at her. "My wife doesn't appreciate me arresting women who haven't done anything wrong."

"I can pull the blonde's hair. Will that get me arrested?"

Weston sidles up to me. "Let's get out of here before the women start a riot for the chance to get arrested by you."

I glare at him. "I'm married, remember? You were at my wedding two days ago."

"Congratulations," Agent Ashford says.

"Thanks."

Weston rolls his eyes. "Are you making friends with our detainees?"

I snort. "Oh please. You would have picked up Tammi if this were the *Bootlegger* bar."

"I can pick up whoever I want. I'm not a married man."

"Your loss."

Agent Ashford smiles up at me. "Your wife is a lucky woman."

I grin. "I'm the lucky one."

And I am lucky.

Chloe could have checked out now that we're married. But she woke up this morning hours before she needed to go to work to help out. She even took Natalia to summer camp before she had a chance to have breakfast. Not many women would do what she did.

Chloe makes the perfect wife.

Too bad our marriage isn't real.

Chapter 17

Mermaid Mini Golf – an excuse to drink beer and whiskey

CHLOE

Sophia sticks her head in my office. "Let's go."

"Go where? Drunk poker isn't tonight."

She rolls her eyes. "Duh. It's Mermaid Mini Golf night."

I nearly groan. Mermaid Mini Golf is a monthly tradition I started. Since my friends and I were all beyond busy trying to get *Five Fathoms Brewing* up and running, we didn't spend much leisure time together. I missed my friends and insisted on this new tradition.

And now I'm regretting it. Tonight is one of the few evenings I have off. I want to spend it with Lucas and Natalia. But I'm not about to confess to my best friend about how I want to spend the night with my fake family.

Although, Lucas and Natalia don't feel fake to me. They feel very, very real. They feel like a promise of something great. Something I don't deserve but wish I could have.

"I can't go. I promised Lucas I'd help Natalia tonight."

Sophia snorts. "It's cute you think you can lie to me."

"I'm not lying."

"You always tap your bottom lip when you're lying."

She points to me and I realize I am indeed tapping my lip. "Sometimes I wish you never moved home."

"Liar. You love me and you know it. Now, switch off your computer and put on your golf shoes, it's time for Mermaid Mini Golf."

"You don't wear golf shoes for mini golf."

"Good." She nods. "You're ready then."

I hold up a hand. "I need to phone Lucas and tell him I won't be home for dinner."

"Hey," Lucas answers the phone. "Are you almost finished? Dinner is nearly ready."

I scowl. I want to be home eating dinner with Lucas and Natalia. Not playing mini golf with my friends.

"Actually, I forgot I have this monthly tradition to play mini golf with my friends."

He chuckles. "I'll warn the on-duty officer."

"Hey now. I'm not always getting in trouble."

"And Natalia won't throw a fit when I force her to eat cauliflower tonight."

"Ugh. Gross. Cauliflower."

"Have fun. I'll see you when you get home."

Home. I love the idea of Lucas and Natalia being my home. Of going home to them every night. Of spending every evening with them watching silly programs on television. Of waking up every morning knowing they're in the house and I'm not alone.

Although, I would prefer to wake up next to Lucas every morning. I've fantasized about his naked chest more than is healthy. I've dreamed about exploring his skin with my tongue every night. The man is a star in my dreams.

"What's the holdup?" Nova asks as she barges into my office with Maya on her heels.

"Judging by the dreamy look on Chloe's face, she's thinking about Lucas," Maya says.

"She was talking to him on the phone," Sophia whisper-shouts.

I stand. "I thought we were playing mini golf."

Maya claps. "I love this. Lucas and Chloe are cute together. They make the perfect couple."

"We're not a couple," I remind her *and* myself. "Our marriage isn't real."

"It seemed awful real when you were glued to him while dancing at your wedding reception," Sophia says.

There's no explaining to my friends who have love on the brain. I herd them out of my office and down the hallway to the rear exit.

"Where's Paisley?"

Nova points to Paisley standing in front of Sophia's car with her putter in her hand. Damn. Mermaid Mini Golf is halfway across the island near *Mermaid Mystical Gardens*. I'm never going to make it home in time to say goodnight to Natalia if I don't have my own transportation.

But my car is in my garage back home. There's no way my friends are going to let me go pick it up. I might as well make the best of the situation.

I force a smile on my face. "You can use your own putter as much as you want, I'm still going to kick your ass."

"I've been studying YouTube videos." Of course, she has. Paisley hates to lose at anything.

We pile into the car and drive to the mini golf course. It's deserted at this hour. Which is good since our group tends to be a bit loud. Usually, I'm the loud one but I want this game over as quick as possible.

"I'll get the whiskey." Sophia pours shots of whiskey into plastic cups.

Paisley holds up a cooler. "And I've got the beer."

Because you can't play Mermaid Mini Golf without beer and whiskey. We drink a shot of whiskey before we begin. While we're playing, the person with the highest score per hole has to drink from her beer. If you have two high scores in a row, you have to drink a shot of whiskey.

Except I don't want to get drunk. I have no desire to have a hangover while dealing with the morning chaos of Natalia. Plus, I have a slight tendency to run my mouth when I'm drunk. I don't need to be a genius to figure out my friends want all the details on Lucas.

They can keep wanting. I'm not telling. Good thing I can be sneaky.

I raise my cup of whiskey. "Here's to the bootleggers. Masters of sneaky sips and secret stashes. Thanks for keeping the party alive."

I sip my whiskey but don't drink it all. Especially since Sophia poured me an extra-large amount. If she's trying to be subtle, she's failing.

I wave my putter in the air. "I'm first."

I'm always first since we go in alphabetical order. Which might have been my idea to begin with.

I set my ball down and line up my shot. I draw my putter back and—

"Holy mermaids! Did you see that?" Maya yells.

I ignore her and putt my ball. Excellent. I'm mere inches from the hole. I line up my shot and— Nova stumbles into me.

"Oops. Sorry. Too much whiskey." She pretends to hiccup.

I wait until she dances away and line my shot up again. This time no one stops me.

"Two. Not bad." I dig my ball out of the hole and wait for my friends to take their turns.

None of my friends beat me. Not even Paisley, who looks in pain when she scrunches up her face as she stares at the hole before putting.

"I always lose," Maya complains when she has to drink.

Nova smiles. "But you're having fun!" My friend can always see the bright side. It would be amazing if it weren't annoying.

"Until the next morning when you guys message me all the stuff I did the previous night."

Sophia wraps an arm around Maya's shoulders. "We're helping you break out of your shy persona."

"Being shy isn't a handicap," Maya mutters.

"But it does stop you from taking a chance on Caleb."

Maya's cheeks darken. "Caleb is a friend. Nothing more."

"But you want more," Nova says.

"We're not discussing me. We're supposed to be bugging Chloe about Lucas tonight." Maya's eyes widen when she realizes what she said and she slaps a hand over her mouth.

"Don't worry about spilling the beans, Maya. It was kind of obvious what you were up to when you tried to sabotage me on the first hole."

"I told you this plan was silly," Paisley says.

Sophia sticks her tongue out at Paisley. "You say all our plans are silly."

"Because they are."

"Maybe you're a fuddy duddy who needs to lighten up."

Nova waves her hands in the air. "No fighting!"

Paisley's dead serious when she answers. "We're not fighting. We're having a discussion on whether I'm a fuddy duddy or not."

"This sucks. Chloe is on to us now."

I wag my finger at Sophia. "I wasn't going to give you any dirt on Lucas anyway."

She crosses her arms over her chest and pouts. "I don't know why not. I told you everything about me and Flynn."

"Liar!"

"Shush," Maya hisses. "We'll get kicked out again."

"We're not getting kicked out because I'm not talking."

"Does this mean we can go?" Paisley asks. "I'm working on a new recipe for a session IPA. It's nearly ready to taste test."

Awesome. I can get home in time to say goodnight to Natalia. Maybe read her a chapter of the Enola Holmes mystery she's reading. Cuddling with Natalia in bed while reading to her is my new favorite thing. It's better than Five Fathoms Summer IPA, which says a lot.

"Let's get Paisley back to the brewery." I herd everyone toward the exit. "We don't want the session IPA wasted. Clients have been asking if we have one."

Sophia tugs on my hand. "Who are you and what have you done with our Chloe?"

Cindy, the teenager on duty, bustles toward us before I can answer. Thank goodness because I'm not ready to confess to Sophia about how lonely I am. How I hide my loneliness behind my wild child persona. How Lucas fills holes I didn't think could ever be filled.

"Are you leaving?" Cindy asks.

We hand her our putters and balls. "Thank the Kraken. We had a lottery to decide who had to work tonight. I lost. I thought I'd have to kick you out again."

Paisley's nose wrinkles. "You've never kicked us out. We've been politely asked to vacate the premises before is all."

I hurry to Sophia's car. We'll be here all night debating about the difference between being kicked out and being asked to vacate the premises if Paisley has anything to do about it.

But I don't have the time. I can't wait to see Natalia and Lucas again. I have a feeling I'll never spend enough time with those two.

Chapter 18

Family night – may involve teasing and poker but always involves whiskey

LUCAS

I groan as I lower myself onto the sofa. I'm exhausted. I thought being a small town cop would be relaxing. I didn't realize Smuggler's Hideaway isn't a typical small town island. If I had, I might not have spent the day arresting women for exposing themselves at the *Bootlegger* bar.

Weston thought it was hilarious. He also ended up asking one of the women out to dinner. Personally, I don't understand the appeal of a woman who throws herself at you. I much prefer a complicated woman.

Chloe skips down the stairs. Speaking of complicated women.

"You ready?"

"The game doesn't start for fifteen minutes."

She rolls her eyes. "Not the game. Are you ready for drunk poker?"

"Drunk poker?"

"I told you it's family night."

Shit. I forgot. "Drunk poker is family night?"

"Lily tried doing a monthly Sunday dinner but people kept on cancelling. No one cancels on drunk poker."

I draw a hand down my beard. I'm tired and have no desire to go anywhere, let alone move from the couch. Natalia is at a friend's house for dinner and a movie. I thought I had the evening to relax.

"I'm sorry, Chloe. But can I skip this one time?"

"You want to skip this one time?"

I nod. "Yeah. It's been a hell of a day."

"So, this is how it works?"

"How what works?" I ask, although I sense I'm walking into a trap.

"I do everything I can to help your family but you won't spend one night with mine."

I cringe. She's right. She has done everything for me. But there's one flaw in her reasoning.

"Lily and Jack aren't your real family."

"How dare you?" She growls. "How dare you say the two adults who helped me to survive my childhood aren't my family? Do you have any clue what my childhood was like?"

Shit. I fucked up. I stand and prowl toward her. "No, I don't. Because you won't tell me."

"Because I don't want to talk about it! Would you want to discuss how your mother bullied you? How she starved you? How she locked you in a closet if you didn't behave?"

My heart seizes at the pain in her voice. "Your mother did what?"

"You want details? I'll give you details. She forced me to compete in beauty pageants from the time I was five. I hated those pageants. Everything was about your outer appearance. Why do you think I hate being called beautiful?"

A tear slips from her eye and I wipe it away. "We don't have to discuss this."

I don't want her in pain. I never want Chloe to ever feel pain.

"Too bad. You started this. I'm ending it. Whenever I lost a pageant, Mom was convinced it was because I was too fat. I was six years old and she'd starve me. She would send me to school without a lunch and claim I forgot mine at home. It's hard to forget something that never existed."

"Sophia shared her lunches with me. I don't know if Lily figured out what was happening, but Sophia's lunches grew until she basically had enough food for two."

I don't ask why she didn't tell anyone. I've seen enough abused kids in my job to know it's not a simple question with a simple answer. A manipulative parent can make the child feel as if it's her fault she's being punished.

"Okay," I murmur as I wrap my arms around her. Her knees buckle and she melts into me. I'll be her strength whenever she needs it. "I'll go to drunk poker but I'm not getting drunk."

She pushes away from me. "It's not your choice to get drunk or not. It's about your poker skills."

I waggle my eyebrows. "Don't you worry. I've got the skills."

Her eyes flare but she clears her throat and steps back. "You'll have to prove it."

I motion toward the door. "Let's go."

Lily and Jack's house is less than five minutes from mine. Nothing is far in Smuggler's Rest. I was afraid I'd find the small town suffocating. But it's not. I glance over at Chloe. It's intriguing.

"Awesome!" Weston hollers when we enter his parents' house, which is already crowded with most of Chloe's family. "I win the jackpot."

I glare at him. "Stop making bets about me."

"Don't get your panties in a twist. It's just a bit of fun."

"It's fun at Chloe's expense. Not okay."

"Chloe?" He raises an eyebrow. "You're worried about the wild child?"

Chloe cringes next to me. She doesn't enjoy being referred to as the wild child. What she doesn't enjoy, she doesn't have to endure.

I squeeze her shoulder before stalking toward Weston. "I told you to stop referring to my wife as a wild child."

"You don't have to call her your wife in this house. Everyone knows the marriage is a sham."

A sham? I growl. Our marriage is not a sham. It's real. Chloe and I *are* married. We said our vows, we exchanged rings, and we had our first dance. It's real.

"Do you want me to choke you out again?" I ask instead of arguing with him about my marriage. My marriage is not his business. It's no one's business but mine and Chloe's.

"I am loving this!" Sophia shouts.

Her boyfriend, Flynn, wraps an arm around her and hauls her close. "Don't encourage them."

"Weston is my big brother. I'm legally obligated to root for him getting his ass kicked."

"He's also my best friend," Flynn says.

The door flies open and Nova rushes in. "Am I late? Am I the last one to arrive? What did I miss?"

"Weston and Lucas are about to throw down. It's so romantic." Maya sighs. "Lucas is fighting for Chloe."

Chloe marches forward and shoves me away from Weston. "Enough. No one's fighting for anyone."

Jack clears his throat. "I don't know. I think Lucas should have to fight for you." He narrows his eyes on me. "Lucas didn't ask me for your hand in marriage."

Aw crap. I didn't realize how close Chloe was to Jack and Lily until fifteen minutes ago. Had I known, I would have asked him for her hand in marriage.

"No one is asking anyone for my hand in marriage. I am my own woman and I can make decisions for myself," Chloe says.

Paisley pushes her glasses up her nose. "I have to agree with Chloe on this one. The practice of asking a woman's father for her hand in marriage is anachronistic at its best, patriarchal at its worst."

"I think it's romantic," Maya says.

Paisley purses her lips. "It's romantic for a woman to be a possession? Because that's where the tradition comes from. A father had to give his daughter permission to leave the family home."

"Why are you raining on my romantic parade?" Maya wails.

"Because there's nothing romantic about a woman being chattel."

"True," Lily agrees. "We need to organize another women's rights march."

"Are they serious?" I ask Weston. I'm not sure how we went from my marriage being a sham to organizing a women's rights march.

"Yep. Mom loves to organize rallies. But don't worry. She never makes the men carry the sign saying *Fuck the Patriarchy*."

I choke. "Excuse me? Carry a sign?"

He slaps me on the shoulder. "You married into the family, bro. This is what our family does."

"I thought we were here to play poker."

He grins. "I love when virgins join the family."

I cross my arms over my chest. "I'm not a virgin."

"In this family, you are." He claps his hands. "Who's ready to play some poker?"

We make our way to the dining room table which is set up for poker. Lily hands out shots of whiskey.

She raises her glass. "To the smugglers, bootleggers, rum-runners."

"And the mermaids who loved them," everyone except me responds.

Chloe elbows me. "Drink your shot."

I down the shot. I expect the whiskey to burn but it's smooth. "This is good."

"It's Buccaneer's whiskey," Lily says.

"Buccaneer's whiskey? Is everything on this island named after a mermaid or related to Prohibition?

"Don't worry. You'll get used to it," she says. "And we'll help. It's what families do. Help each other."

Family? Despite my arguing about how my marriage to Chloe is real, it's not a forever marriage. And her family is not mine.

But I wish they were. I have my parents but I don't have any siblings or cousins or aunts and uncles.

I glance around the table at the size of the group. I always wanted a big family. And I wanted to give Natalia a big family, too.

My gaze catches on Chloe. I want her to be my family. I nearly fall off my chair from the realization.

Too bad my focus needs to be on Natalia and keeping her safe.

Chapter 19

Phone – handy little gadget which only works if you actually answer it

Chloe

> **Lucas: Can you pick Natalia up from camp? Running late.**

I check the time. I should be able to walk over to the summer camp before the kids are finished.

> **No problem!**

I leave my bike at *Five Fathoms Brewing* and walk over to the camp. When I arrive, the kids are just finishing up. I lean against the fence and wait for Natalia. She comes rushing out holding another girl's hand.

"Chloe! You're here!"

I hug her in greeting. "Your dad got caught up at work."

"I could have walked home on my own."

I agree but Lucas is a bit overprotective. I assume once he gets used to Smuggler's Hideaway he'll loosen the reins a bit. In the meantime, it's my job to stand united with him.

I tweak her nose. "Maybe next time."

She rolls her eyes. "Maybe means no."

"I didn't say no."

"Parents always say maybe when they mean no."

Parents? Does she consider me one of her parents? I'd love to be her parent.

Slow your mermaid loving heart, Chloe. Natalia is not your child. You are not a step-mom. This marriage is not real. No matter how much you may wish it was.

"I'll speak to your dad about it. It's the best offer I've got." I hold out my hand and we shake on it.

She giggles. "You're silly."

"Ask her," the girl with Natalia whispers in a loud voice.

I smile at her. "I'm Chloe."

"This is Piper," Natalia introduces. "She's my friend."

"Nice to meet you, Piper. What is Natalia supposed to ask me?"

Natalia clears her throat. "Can I have a sleepover at Piper's house? Please. Please. Please. I used to have sleepovers all the time back home."

Shoot. What do I do? Do I need to check with Lucas? I probably should.

"Let me check with your dad." I dial Lucas's number but he doesn't pick up. Darn it. What now?

A woman who appears slightly familiar joins us. "Chloe?"

"August?" I guess.

"I didn't know if you'd remember me. I was several classes ahead of you."

"Smuggler's Hideaway," I murmur as if naming the island is an answer for everything.

"I heard you married Natalia's dad." She grins. "You snatched up the hottie police officer awful quick."

My brow furrows. "Aren't you married?"

"Yep. Married my high school sweetheart when I got pregnant with this one." She wraps an arm around Piper. "Been married ever since. But I can still look." She winks. "And the whole island is devastated you snatched Lucas up before anyone else got a chance to play with him."

She has no idea. There's no playing happening between me and Lucas.

"Mom." Piper tugs on August's arm. "Ask her."

"My daughter, who has forgotten the magic word despite how many times I've reminded her, wants to have Natalia over tonight for a sleepover. Is that okay?"

What do I do? Do I try to contact Lucas again? Will it appear suspicious if I need his permission? Will rumors spread about our marriage being a hoax? Everyone's already gossiping about how fast we got married.

Here goes nothing.

"Will you be home the entire evening?" I ask. She nods. "Do you have a list of Natalia's allergies?"

"All the parents received a list of allergies of each kid at the start of the summer camp."

"And you have my phone number if anything goes wrong?"

She giggles. "Or I can just run over to your house."

She could. No one's too far away in Smuggler's Rest. In fact, no one's too far away on the island of Smuggler's Hideaway.

I kneel in front of Natalia. "Do you promise to let me know if anything goes wrong? Anything at all? It doesn't matter what time of night it is. I won't be mad."

"Does this mean I can stay over with Piper?"

I blow out a breath and take a risk. "Yes."

She squeals and jumps up and down. "Thank you, Chloe!"

Piper and her rush off without a backward glance. "Doesn't she need clothes?"

"She has her bag of spare clothes with her."

Oh right. I forgot one of the requirements of summer camp was to have a set of spare clothes since getting dirty isn't a rare occurrence.

August pats my arm. "It's hard the first time they're away, but trust me, you'll be happy to have the night to yourself. Enjoy it. Once you get pregnant, it's all downhill."

I frown at her. Once I get pregnant? I'm not getting pregnant. I'm never having children.

"Thanks. If Natalia's a bother, feel free to send her home."

She waves as she rushes to follow the girls.

Once she's out of hearing range, I ring Lucas again. He still doesn't pick up. He must be dealing with an emergency. He wouldn't ignore me for any other reason. Not when he knows I'm with Natalia.

By the time Lucas returns home a few hours later, I'm fighting off panic. My mind knows nothing happened to him.

Someone would have contacted me if he were injured or in the hospital.

My heart disagrees. My heart wants to know what could have possibly kept Lucas busy for three hours and unable to return a simple phone call.

"Hey!" Lucas calls in greeting.

"Hey? I'll hey you. Where have you been? Have you forgotten how a phone works? Do you need me to give you a course? It's not difficult. It starts with picking up your phone when it rings."

He rubs a hand over his beard. "Shit. Sorry. A herd of sheep got loose and wreaked havoc on half the island."

"A group of sheep is a flock. And how long does it take to get the sheep under control?"

"When your partner is Weston, a long ass time."

I blow out a breath. This isn't me. I don't lose my mind when a man ghosts me.

"What happened?"

"A farmer was replacing his fence and a sheep got out. Did you know where one sheep goes the rest follow?"

I giggle. I actually do know that. I also know I will never pull a prank involving sheep ever again. Give me a raccoon any day. They'll do anything for food.

"Every single time we thought we had all of the sheep corralled in the correct location, one of them would get a hair up his ass and escape. And the rest of the flock would follow."

"You look pretty good for someone who spent the past three hours chasing after sheep."

"I showered at the station. Shit. I should have called you back then. I'm so used to my mom and dad knowing about the job and how I can be late, I didn't think to check my phone and make sure everything went well with picking up Natalia." He glances around. "Where is she anyway?"

"She's at a sleepover with her friend, Piper."

He freezes. "What did you say?"

"Did all the bleating affect your ears?"

A muscle in his jaw ticks. "I can't believe you let Natalia go to a sleepover."

"Are you mad?"

"Hell yeah, I am."

"Why? I don't understand what you're this mad about. I checked with Piper's parents. They will be home all night. They have a list of Natalia's allergies and all of our phone numbers."

"Because Natalia is *my* daughter. Not yours."

Pain slices through me at his words. He's right. Natalia isn't mine. This is a game we're playing to appease his ex. None of it is real.

But I don't back down. I never do.

I poke his chest. "How would it have looked if I said I couldn't give Natalia permission? Huh? We're supposed to be married. I'm supposed to be her stepmother. Do stepmothers have no rights?"

He captures my hand. "You're not Natalia's stepmother, though, are you?"

Kick me while I'm down, will you? News flash. This girl doesn't stay down for long.

I glare at him. "Don't you dare blame me. If you would have just answered your phone, I could have checked with you."

"Now, it's my fault?"

"Yes, you big buffoon. You can't ask me to help out with Natalia and then get mad when I give her permission to sleep over at a friend's house. It's one or the other. I help or I'm not involved. What do you want? Do you want me to move back into my house?"

He growls before using his hold on my hand to haul me near. I slam into his chest with an oomph.

"Stop talking."

"I can—"

I don't manage to finish my sentence before his lips slam down on mine. His kiss is hard. But I don't care. The feel of his lips against mine is all I need. If this is supposed to be punishment, I'm going to be bad more often. Maybe all the time.

He thrusts his tongue into my mouth and I suck on it. He tastes of musk, mint, and man. It's a heady combination. It's the taste I remember from our wedding day. One I've imagined ever since.

He moans and presses his hard cock against my stomach. I gasp at the feel of his hard length against me.

"I'm going to fuck that attitude right out of you."

My entire body goes up in flames at his declaration. "You can try."

He throws me over his shoulder.

I should probably stop him. This is a bad idea. Trust me. I know. I'm an expert at bad ideas. But I couldn't stop him now if I wanted to.

And make no mistake about it. I don't want to.

Chapter 20

Bad decision – when you do something you shouldn't, but you really, really want to

LUCAS

Chloe bounces on my shoulder as I bound up the stairs. I keep my arm wrapped around her waist to keep her right where I want her.

This is wrong. We agreed to keep our marriage professional. I should drop Chloe in her room and lock myself away from her.

But I'm not going to. Not when my cock has been aching to be inside this woman since the first time I saw her. I've imagined her long legs wrapped around my waist while I plunge my cock inside her too many times to stop now.

I hurry into my room. I want Chloe's scent on my sheets. If this is the one time I have her, I want to be able to lay in my bed at night and remember how she looked in *my* room in *my* bed while I gave her pleasure she won't be able to forget.

I throw Chloe on the bed and she giggles as she bounces. "I thought I was supposed to be the wild one."

"You drive me wild, wildcat."

And she does. I usually keep a tight rein on my emotions. It's a necessity when you're a cop and walk in on a woman who's been beaten bloody by her husband.

But with Chloe, I can't help myself. She makes me crazy with desire to rip her clothes off. To touch her slight curves. To kiss her skin. To bury myself inside her.

I inhale a deep breath before I decide to hell with control and do all the things I've been fantasizing about in my shower with my cock in my hand since I discovered my definition of temptation lived next door.

I plant a knee on the bed and fall forward onto my fists above her. Her eyes flare and she licks her bottom lip. Stay on track, Lucas.

"This doesn't change anything," I growl since I'm no longer capable of normal speech.

She raises her eyebrows. "This as in sex?"

I growl. "Yes, sex."

"Gotcha."

I hesitate. Is she lying? In my experience, women have a hard time distinguishing between sex and love. I should probably walk out the door. I'm not going to, though.

"I'm serious, wildcat. This is sex and only sex."

Her nose wrinkles. "I wouldn't describe this as sex. No one's naked. There's no panting. I..."

I tickle her ribs before she can continue. She tries to squirm away from me, but I don't let her go. I never want to let her go. *Just sex, Lucas. Just sex.*

"Stop!" She bats my hands away but she's giggling too hard to be very effective.

I stop tickling her ribs and glide my hands up and down her sides. "Well, well, well, my wildcat is ticklish. I'm filing this information away for future use."

"You better not tell anyone I'm ticklish."

I freeze. "Or what?"

She wags her finger at me. "Nuh-uh. No way. I'm not revealing my bag of pranks to an officer of the law."

I chuckle. "Bag of pranks? Is this an actual bag?"

"I'm never telling."

I lift my hands and wiggle my fingers. "What if I tickle you more?"

"Cruel and unusual punishment, Officer Fellows."

I glide my hand along her ribs until I reach the swell of her breast. "What if I tease you in another way?"

Her breath hitches. "What way?"

I bend over to whisper in her ear. "I don't let you come for a long, long time." I bite her earlobe and she shivers. I love how responsive she is to me. I can't wait to see how long I need to tease her before she's screaming my name in ecstasy.

Speaking of which. I sit up and grasp the hem of her t-shirt. "This okay?"

She lifts her hands above her head. "More than okay. Please feel free to do whatever you want to my body without asking again." Her nose wrinkles. "Except no butthole stuff. It's an exit only zone."

I bark out a laugh. I've never laughed while in bed with a woman before. But I like it.

Except I don't want Chloe to be able to speak. I want her gasping with pleasure. Begging me to let her come.

My cock presses against my zipper. It's on board with this plan.

I whip her t-shirt off leaving Chloe in a white lace bra. Her pink nipples are visible through the lace. It's an invitation I can't resist. I trace my finger around her nipple and she arches her back to push her chest closer to me.

I watch as her nipple hardens for me. "Is this what you wear underneath your clothes every day?"

"Do you not approve?"

"Don't beg for compliments."

"Or what? Are you going to spank me? Or maybe handcuff me?"

I still. "Are you serious? You want me to handcuff you?"

She shrugs. "I've never been handcuffed before, but I feel safe trying it with you. You are a police officer after all."

Warmth stabs me in the chest before spreading throughout my body. She feels safe with me? After everything her mom put her through? She feels safe. I vow she will always feel safe with me.

"Maybe next time," I grumble.

There shouldn't be a next time. This time shouldn't be happening as it is. But I can't stop myself from promising this woman everything she wants. She's my wildcat. She's mine to protect. To pleasure.

Speaking of pleasure…

"The bra can stay on but the rest of your clothes have got to go." She reaches for her pants but I stop her. "My job."

She lifts her hands to grab the headboard. "You won't hear me complaining."

She won't be able to speak at all if it's up to me. And it is up to me. I'm the one in this bed with her. I'm the one who's going to make her mad for passion. Starting now. Talking time is done.

I rip her pants open and slide the zipper down to reveal a pair of white lacy panties to match her white lacy bra. Damn. I'm going to imagine her in this outfit whenever she walks around the house from now on. I thought she was torturing me before but that was before I knew about her lingerie.

I shove her pants down her legs until she can kick the material off. My wildcat is a vision in her lacy lingerie with her porcelain skin on display and her auburn hair spread out over my pillow. I'm tempted to snatch a picture.

My cock presses against my zipper to remind me this isn't the time for picture taking. This is the time for memory making.

I whip my t-shirt over my head and she gasps. "Holy mermaids."

"No mermaids. Just me."

She reaches to touch me but I stop her. "Hands back on the headboard."

If she touches me now, I won't be able to go slow. And I want to take my time since this is the one and only time my wife will be in this bed.

I glide my hands up Chloe's thighs and she automatically widens her legs for me. The sight of my tanned oversized hands on her alabaster skin has me fixated. The goosebumps following in the wake of my movement intrigue me.

"Are you going to torture me all night?"

"I did warn you I would tease you."

"Two can play at this game." She wraps her legs around my waist and rubs her panties clad core against my stomach. I can feel her wet excitement through her panties.

"Are you wet for me?"

"Are you hard for me?"

"Oh, Chloe. I'm always hard for you."

"Same, hubby. Same."

I scowl at her use of the word hubby. This isn't real. We can't get attached. As soon as Holly drops her custody suit, Chloe and I will return to being nothing more than neighbors.

I wish it could be otherwise but I can't chance it. I already had one wife who wouldn't stick. The wild child's chances of sticking are even worse.

Chloe's heels rub against my back to remind me this is not the time for contemplation. This is my chance to feel her squeeze my cock when she comes. To watch her face when ecstasy hits.

I unwind her legs from around me. "Are you ready for me?"

She widens her legs and I dive a hand into her panties. I skip her clit and go straight for her pussy. I plunge two fingers inside. I groan at how hot and wet she is.

I pump in and out a few times and Chloe moans as her walls flutter around my fingers. Not good enough. I want to feel her pussy clamp down on my cock.

I remove my fingers and she hisses. "Why did you stop? I'm nearly there."

"Because you're not coming until my cock is buried deep inside you."

Her breath hitches. "Okay."

I slide her panties off her before standing to push my jeans down. My cock juts out and points straight at Chloe. It knows what it wants.

I dive into the top drawer of my nightstand. I hope to hell I have some condoms in here. I find a box and dig one out. Once the protection is secured, I climb back into bed.

I settle between Chloe's thighs and hitch my cock at her entrance. "Are you ready for this?"

"I've been re—"

I don't let her finish before I sink inside her. Fuck. Fuck. Fuck. She feels better than I could have ever imagined. My cock is ready to explode. I clench my jaw and inhale a breath through my nose. I will not come until Chloe has screamed my name at least once.

She wraps her legs around my waist and arches her back until her chest hits mine. The feel of her lace against my skin is incredible. But next time, I want to feel her hard nipples pressing against me.

"My wildcat is impatient," I grumble before slowly retreating until only the tip is inside her. "You want wild? I can give you wild."

I surge into her before beginning to pump in and out of her faster and faster until I'm practically rutting inside her.

Chloe's hands grasp my shoulders and her fingernails dig into my skin. "Yes," she hisses. "Harder."

I get to my knees and throw her legs over my shoulders. "My wildcat wants harder, she gets harder."

Her breasts bounce with my thrusts and she claws at the bedsheets as her head twists from side to side. Her walls flutter.

"Are you close?" I don't wait for a reply before sneaking my hand between us to touch her clit. I rub it in circles until Chloe is panting.

"Yes, yes, yes."

"You say my name when you come." I pinch her clit and she explodes.

"Lucas!"

Her walls clamp down on me and I'm helpless to stop my orgasm. It barrels down on me and I growl. "Chloe."

I continue to thrust into her until her body is boneless. I drop her legs and roll to my side.

"W-w…" she stutters.

I chuckle. "Did I cause the wild child to become speechless?"

She slaps my stomach. "Catching my breath is all."

I twist my head to glance at her. She has a tiny smile on her face and drops of sweat bead her forehead. She's never looked more beautiful.

Too bad she's not destined to be mine.

She's a flight risk. And I can't take risks with Natalia.

No matter how much I might want to. I'm afraid I've never wanted anything else in my life as much as I want Chloe.

Chapter 21

Run – what happens when you're a scaredy-cat

CHLOE

I wake surrounded by the smell of sex and an arm banded around my waist. This is a first. Usually, when I have sex, I skedaddle before the cuddling can begin. I am not a cuddler.

Except I'm literally lying in a bed with Lucas's arm around me while he spoons me from behind. And I am as close to him as I possibly can be.

Lucas has the ability to cause me to make decisions I would never usually make. Such as sleeping with my fake husband who I want to be a real husband.

I slap a hand over my mouth to stop my gasp from being audible. I want Lucas to be my real husband. Holy mermaids in the ocean. I'm falling in love with Lucas.

This is unacceptable. I can't fall in love with my husband. This is fake and he doesn't want anything real. He made *that* perfectly obvious when he made me agree sex wouldn't change our relationship last night.

Maybe I can change his mind. Maybe I can turn on all the charm and convince Lucas to give me a chance.

Except I can't. Lucas is the kind of man who will want more children. And I will never have children.

Damnit, Chloe. I've been in some shitty situations before, although the time I got stuck in the cave without any clothes was totally not my fault, but this is the worst. The absolute worst.

There's only one thing I can do.

Run.

I lift Lucas's arm and scooch out from underneath him. He grunts before rolling over. Phew.

I tiptoe toward the door gathering my clothes as I go. Thank goodness Natalia is at a sleepover. I wouldn't want her to catch me doing the walk of shame naked down the hallway. She'd be scarred for life.

No matter how much she claims to want me and her dad to get together. Sex between your parents is always icky. I assume. I wouldn't know since my dad disappeared before I could form memories.

I debate not showering, but I can smell the sex on my skin. I shower as fast as I can before throwing on clothes and hurrying out of the house.

I wish I could say I'm exaggerating but I'm gasping for breath by the time I start cycling toward *Five Fathoms Brewing.* I don't have any other choice. I can't get attached to a man who doesn't want me. I know how it feels to have a mother who doesn't want you. I couldn't pick my mom, but I can pick my man.

The brewery is locked up tight when I arrive. Probably because it's Saturday morning and the offices are closed. The bar and restaurant will be open later for lunch and dinner, which is my excuse for being here.

I'm finishing up the payroll when the door bursts open and Sophia, Nova, Maya, and Paisley tumble inside.

"What are you doing here? It's Saturday."

Sophia snorts. "What are we doing here?"

"It wasn't a rhetorical question."

Nova smiles. "But it was kind of silly. You know why we're here."

My brow wrinkles. "I do?"

Paisley sighs. "Addy phoned. She said you were being bitchy to clients."

"I haven't been bitchy to clients. I've been in this office doing paperwork."

"You didn't tell a client you were going to shove him off the cliffs at *Mermaid Mystical Gardens?*" Nova asks.

I wave away her question. "It was a misunderstanding. He called me a witch and asked me where my broom was. I told him if he wants to fly, he can fly off a cliff."

"You can't be mean to clients no matter if they're jerks or not," Sophia declares.

"I..." I pause when Maya sniffs me. "What are you doing?"

"I'm examining the beard rash on your neck. I wonder how far down it goes." She reaches for my shirt but I bat her away.

"Don't start seeing romance where it doesn't exist."

"I happily admit to being a romantic, and this romantic especially enjoys the sexy, smutty scenes and can spot beard rash a mile away." She points at me. "You had sex with Lucas."

Nova claps. "Yes! I knew Lucas was perfect for her."

"Calm your tits, Ms. Sunshine and Ms. Romantic. Nothing's changed between us."

Sophia points at me. "But you did have sex."

"Sex is sex. We agreed it wouldn't change our relationship."

Maya rolls her eyes. "Sex always changes a relationship."

"In a good way," Nova sings.

"Actually," Paisley begins.

Sophia holds up her palm. "No. No statistics about relationships going sour because of sex or whatever nerd fact you're going to pull out of your ass."

Paisley's nose wrinkles. "I do not keep facts in my ass."

"We should go out to celebrate," Nova suggests and everyone nods in agreement.

"The Bootlegger Escape Room festival is this weekend. Whoever escapes the fastest, drinks free for the rest of the night. Who's in?" Sophia asks and everyone except me raises their hand.

"I am not celebrating having sex with Lucas."

Maya huffs. "We're not celebrating you having sex. We're celebrating the beginning of your love story."

I feign gagging. "No love for me. Just banging. Lots and lots of banging."

"Does this mean you're going to give us details about Lucas?" Sophia pulls me out of my chair and drags me to the door. "I want to know everything."

"I'm not giving you details."

"Please," Maya begs. "The book I'm reading is a clean romance. I didn't realize there was no sex in it at all. But now I'm halfway through and I have to finish it. I feel as if I've gone celibate."

"You should watch porn," Paisley suggests.

I screech to a halt. "What did you say?"

"She should watch porn." Paisley glances around at our group of friends, all of whom have their mouths hanging open. "Why is everyone surprised? Women can watch porn."

I groan. "Someone stop her before she goes on a feminist rant."

Nova grasps Paisley's hand. "We realize women can watch porn, sweetie. The thing we're confused about is you watching porn."

Paisley wrenches her hand away. "Being a nerd does not mean I don't have sexual needs and desires. In fact, sexual satisfaction—"

"Nope." I slap a hand over her mouth. "I'm not listening to a scientific lecture about sex. It'll ruin my post sex high."

My post sex high evaporated the second I realized I was falling for Lucas, but I am never ever admitting my feelings to my friends. Maya would have a honeymoon booked before I had the chance to explain Lucas doesn't want what I want out of our 'marriage'.

"I love this!" Maya shouts. Several people in the parking lot look over and her face darkens until her cheeks are red. "Sorry," she whispers.

"I knew we'd be the fastest through the escape room," Sophia says when we enter *Rumrunner* later.

The Bootlegger's Escape Room was a combination of figuring out bootlegger trivia and drinking shots of moonshine. Between Paisley's knowledge of all things and us growing up on moonshine, we were unbeatable.

We find a table and collapse in it. We might have been raised on moonshine, but those five shots are hitting us hard.

"Shots for the winners." The owner of the bar, Harper, slams a tray down on the table. "You know the escape room festival was intended for tourists."

Sophia leans to the side as she attempts to shrug. "They didn't make a rule saying we couldn't."

"I reviewed the rules in detail," Paisley announces.

Nova tries to slap her shoulder and ends up hitting her boob. "Oops. Sorry. What cup size are you hiding under those oversized shirts?" Nova lifts up Paisley's shirt but Paisley shoves her out of the booth.

"I'm okay!" Nova yells from the floor where she's now sprawled. "Nothing hurt."

"Harrumph." Maya snort-snores from the corner of the booth where she's slumped over asleep.

"Maybe you don't need any more shots." Harper draws the tray away, but I stop her.

"Nova and Maya drank extra shots so Paisley could keep her mind clear," I explain.

"It wasn't against the rules," Paisley volunteers when Harper glares at her.

Harper sighs. "Smuggler's Hideaway should know better than to have any loopholes in the rules of a festival with the five of you around."

I throw my hands in the air. "Because we are the champions."

Harper shakes her head. "Your poor husbands."

"I'm not married," Sophia shouts after her.

"As good as," Harper yells back.

Sophia grins. "It's true. I'm as good as married to Flynn. He's stuck with me for life."

Lucky her. I am married but my husband wants nothing to do with me. Except have sex and pretend nothing's changed between the two of us. How can nothing be changed after what we experienced together? Or is he used to having awesome sex?

"Is someone going to help me up?" Nova asks from where she's still sprawled on the floor.

Paisley helps Nova to her feet and gets her settled in a chair.

"It's not the moonshine," Nova claims. "It's the speed of the moonshine."

"We had to be fast or else we wouldn't have won," Sophia says.

"Uh huh," Nova mumbles before she slumps over.

"Maybe we should get these two home," Paisley suggests.

"Let them be. They're perfectly fine." I hand out shots giving me and Sophia two glasses to Paisley's one. "To smugglers, bootleggers, rumrunners, and the mermaids who loved them!"

"To the smugglers!" The rest of the bar joins in as I down my two shots. "Do you ever wonder why a speakeasy is called a speakeasy? The speaking is easy. Finding it is the hard part. Why wasn't it a hardtofind? Sounds better to me."

"I like it," Sophia says. "It makes sense."

"It makes sense because you've been drinking moonshine all day," Paisley says.

Harper arrives and sets another tray of moonshine shots down on our table. "Courtesy of the boys over there." She points to a table of men on the other side of the room. "I explained you're drinking for free but they insisted."

I stand. "I guess I better go thank them personally."

Sophia latches onto me. "No, don't go. Lucas won't appreciate you talking to strange men in a bar."

I push her off of me. "Lucas won't care because nothing's changed."

Lucas and I aren't a real couple. No matter how many times he rocked my world last night. No matter how I woke up feeling safe and protected in his arms.

No matter how much I want otherwise.

Chapter 22

Protective – how Lucas should not feel about his fake wife

LUCAS

I wake and even before I open my eyes, I know she's gone. I knew it. Chloe *is* a runner.

This is why I have to keep my distance from her. This is why our marriage will never be real. I can't risk another woman abandoning me or my daughter.

Except I didn't keep my distance last night. I spent the night buried deep inside her. And when we were both too tired to move, I wrapped my arms around her and ordered her to sleep.

I'm an idiot.

The door bangs open. Is she back? Did she go pick us up breakfast and coffee?

"Dad! Are you here?"

What was I thinking? Of course, Chloe isn't back.

Enough of this bullshit contemplation. My daughter needs me to be there for her. Especially since Chloe isn't here. I feel a twinge of guilt at how upset Chloe was when I reminded her Natalia is my daughter.

I guess we both needed the reminder.

"Dad!" My door flies open. "Are you still in bed? I've been up for hours. We made pancakes for breakfast and went to the beach to eat them. Why don't we ever go to the beach? I want to learn to surf. How old do you have to be to surf?"

"Slow down, cupcake. Did you drink coffee, too?"

"Don't be silly, dad. Kids don't drink coffee."

I start to slide out of bed before I remember I'm naked. This is the problem with Chloe. She makes me lose my mind. Makes me forget my priority is and always will be Natalia.

"Why don't you put your clothes in the laundry room and I'll get dressed and we can decide what to do for the day?"

"Where's Chloe?" she asks instead of complying. "Chloe! Why isn't she answering?"

"Maybe she's still asleep," I lie since I have no intention of explaining to my twelve-year-old what actually happened.

"I'll find her." She rushes off and I grab a pair of boxer shorts before hurrying to the bathroom.

"Chloe isn't here," Natalia announces when I join her in the kitchen fifteen minutes later. "I called her but her phone is switched off."

Is Chloe hiding from my daughter? Not okay. She can't act like Natalia's mother and then disappear.

"Oh wait. According to the calendar, she's working." Natalia points to the calendar on the refrigerator. It has my shifts and Chloe's working hours on it to help us better plan pick-ups for Natalia.

Hold on. Maybe Chloe didn't run? Maybe she's working? I glance at the clock. It's barely ten in the morning. The brewery doesn't open for lunch until noon on Saturday. It's official. Chloe's a runner.

"What do you want to do today, cupcake?" I ask as I pour myself some coffee.

"Can we go to the beach?"

"Didn't you already go to the beach this morning?"

"But, Dad, I didn't have my swimsuit."

"Let me finish my coffee and eat my breakfast and then we'll go."

"Yeah!" She rushes to me and throws her arms around me. "You're the best dad ever. Although, Piper's dad is pretty cool, too. He works at *Mermaid Mystical Gardens*. He can make the rollercoaster stop if he wants to. Why haven't we gone to *Mermaid Mystical Gardens* yet? Piper says it's fun. They have rollercoasters and lots of rides."

"I thought you wanted to go to the beach today?"

"Oh, right. We'll go to the amusement park when Chloe has a day off. Then, we can go as a family."

My heart aches in my chest. I know Natalia wishes Chloe was her mom but it's not to be. As soon as the custody hearings are over, Chloe will be out of our lives. I ignore the way my stomach dips at the reminder.

I don't need Chloe. All I need is a twelve-year-old girl who is not going to learn to surf anytime soon if I have anything to say about it.

We spend several hours on the beach, swimming in the ocean, throwing a frisbee around, and building elaborate sandcastles.

When Natalia declares she's starving, it's the perfect excuse to leave. We pack everything up and make our way home.

I frown when I notice Chloe's bike is missing. She can't still be at work. She was only planning to work the lunch shift today.

We enter the house and Natalia shouts for Chloe.

"She isn't here," she pouts.

Should I message Chloe? Nah. She's an adult. She can handle herself.

My phone beeps with a message from Weston.

> *Your wife is drunk at Rumrunner.*

Damnit. She better not be causing trouble.

> *We're fighting over who gets to arrest her this time.*

There's no reason to wonder any longer if she's causing trouble. She is.

> *I'll go get my wife.*

> *Thought you would.*

I can practically hear his laughter through the text.

"Natalia." I kneel down in front of my daughter. "I need to pick up Chloe."

"Why? Is she in trouble?"

I hope not. "Will you stay with Mrs. Agatha until we get back?"

"Dad. I'm not a child. I can stay home alone."

"I don't know how long I'll be gone."

"Fine," she huffs. "But I'm researching surfing lessons while I'm there."

Once I drop Natalia at our neighbor's house, I drive to the bar. I take the truck since I don't know if Chloe is in any shape to walk.

I step into the bar and let my eyes adjust to the darkness before searching the space. Chloe's friends are in a corner booth. Maya appears to be sleeping while Nova is giggling uncontrollably. Meanwhile, Sophia and Paisley are deep in conversation.

"I'm telling you," Sophia says as I reach them. "I saw the alien plain as daylight outside my window."

"And how much alcohol had you drunk at this point?" Paisley asks.

"Listen to me. It was an alien."

"Was he green and had antennas for ears?"

"Yes!" Sophia slaps her hand on the table. "I knew it! You saw him, too."

"Yes, I did. On Saturday morning in a cartoon on the television."

I clear my throat. "Where's my wife?"

Sophia sighs. "He says, my wife."

"Chloe is his wife or have you forgotten? How much moonshine have you had?"

"As much as you."

Paisley purses her lips. "Chloe is at the bar."

She points to where Chloe is standing with a group of men. Why the hell is she speaking to a bunch of men? After the night we enjoyed? Who the hell does she think she is?

I prowl across the room. The men notice me and frown. Chloe whirls around to see what they're frowning at. She waves to me and nearly falls over. One of the men catches her.

I wrap my arm around her and pull her away from him. "Keep your hands off my wife."

Chloe pets my chest. "Don't be mad, hubby of mine. I was thanking these gentlemen for buying us moonshine."

"They bought you moonshine?"

She grins up at me. "Yep. We won the Bootlegger's Escape Room festival and now the entire bar is buying us rounds." She leans close to me. "They don't need to buy us rounds. We drink free because we won!"

She throws her arms in the air and falls backward. I tighten my hold on her before she falls.

"I think it's time to go home."

She curls her bottom lip in a pout. "But I'm having fun."

"Yeah, spoilsport," one of the men says. "She's having fun."

I growl at him. "My wife is not having fun with you. She's coming home with me."

Chloe pokes my chest. "I live with him because he's my hubby."

"How much have you had to drink?"

Her eyes get foggy as she counts. "There were five shots at the escape room."

"There were shots at the escape room?"

"Duh." She rolls her eyes and tips backward. I steady her. Again. "This is Smuggler's Hideaway. There's always moonshine at our festivals. Do you drink moonshine? Have you tried any?"

She whirls around but I keep my arm banded across her waist. I'm not letting her go with the predatory look on the faces of the men in this place. They're out of luck. Chloe is coming home with me.

"Harper!" she screams. "Can you get my hubby a shot of moonshine?"

I shake my head at the bartender. "I'm good. I'm driving my wife home now."

Chloe sighs. "I love it when you call me your wife."

She couldn't be more beautiful at this moment. All her guards are down and her light green eyes are shining with happiness. What I wouldn't give to witness her smiling up at me every single day for the rest of my life.

I shove those thoughts away. Chloe isn't a keeper. I already chose one woman who wouldn't stay. I know better than to choose another one.

Chapter 23

Hangover – a concept Chloe is not explaining to her fake stepdaughter

CHLOE

I wake with a sudden jerk. Where am I? Why am I wearing my clothes? And why is my head hanging over the end of the bed? With a bucket on the floor in front of me?

I roll over and my stomach protests. My mouth tastes of moonshine. Moonshine?

Ah, yes. I remember. I played coward and ran from the bed I shared with Lucas and ended up drinking my sorrows away at the *Rumrunner* bar after winning the *Bootlegger Escape Room Festival*.

And the prize for being a walking, talking cliché goes to?

"Choe!" Natalia shouts before banging on my door.

I curl into the fetal position. Maybe if I make myself real small, she won't notice I'm here and go away.

"Chloe! Dad said I couldn't wake you until ten. It's one minute past ten now."

"I'm awake," I croak.

The door flies open and she rushes inside. Note to self. Never answer a child when she's banging on your door.

"Do you want breakfast? I already ate – Dad made pancakes – but I can have a second breakfast. Everyone knows you're allowed to have a second breakfast on Sunday."

I hold up my hand before she jumps on the bed. "No breakfast. And no jumping on the bed."

She screeches to a halt. "Dad lets me jump on his bed."

She's totally lying. There's no way Lucas lets her jump on his bed. I know how to handle this.

"Shall I ask him?"

"Um." She twists her ankle and stares at the ground. "Maybe not."

I snort and end up inhaling the scent of alcohol and sweat. My nose wrinkles. Where is that smell coming from? I sniff again and realize it's me. I need a shower and coffee stat.

"I'm going to shower."

"Shower? But you're wearing your clothes. Didn't you shower already? Or did you sleep in your clothes? Dad says I'm not allowed to sleep in my clothes."

I force myself to sit up. "It was late when I got home last night. I was too tired to change."

"Not an excuse according to Dad."

"Good thing he's not my dad then."

"Where is your dad? Will I meet him? Does he live on the island?"

"New rule. No questions before I've had my first coffee."

She sighs. "Dad's grumpy in the morning, too."

I'm not grumpy. I'm hungover. But I'm not about to explain why I'm feeling like crap to a twelve-year-old.

I manage to stand and weave my way toward the door. "Shower time."

"We'll decide what we're doing for the day when you're ready." Natalia skips away.

Doing for the day? I planned to lay in bed all day. But I guess I'm going to pretend I don't feel as if I'm dying all day. Sounds fun.

Once I've showered and dressed, I feel a bit better. Well enough to journey downstairs for some much needed coffee.

When I walk into the kitchen, Lucas is reading the paper at the table while Natalia works on a puzzle. My heart warms. Damn. What I wouldn't give for this to be my Sunday morning every Sunday for the rest of my life.

But it's not to be. I shake my head and moan. Bad idea.

Lucas chuckles. "Not feeling too great this morning?"

I glare at him. "I'm fine."

"Your throat isn't sore?"

"Why would my throat be sore?"

"From singing ninety-nine bottles of moonshine on the wall at the top of your voice."

I wish I could deny it but singing is one of the tamer things I've done while inebriated.

Natalia giggles. "Chloe's silly. It's ninety-nine bottles of beer on the wall."

"Not on Smuggler's Hideaway, kiddo."

"You're dressed." She bounces in her chair. I wish I had half of her energy. "Can we decide what to do today now?"

I wag a finger at her. "I haven't had my coffee yet."

Lucas motions to the coffeemaker on the kitchen counter. "There's coffee in the pot."

"Thank the mermaids," I mutter before pouring myself a cup. I gulp half of it down before joining them at the table.

"I know what I want to do today!" Natalia announces with a shriek and I grimace.

Lucas nods to the two painkillers and water waiting on the table for me. I grunt in thanks before swallowing the pills. I haven't had a hangover this bad in a long time. Whose bright idea was it to add moonshine shots to an escape room?

"What do you want to do today?" Lucas asks his daughter.

I love how gentle his question is despite how Natalia is shouting at the table. Mom would have punished me for being too loud. She wouldn't have slapped me. Physical violence wasn't her thing. A stay locked in the closet or a day of no food or water would have been more her style.

"I want to go to *Mermaid Mystical Gardens!*"

The idea of spending the day on rides nearly has me throwing up. No way can I handle the amusement park today.

"Not today, squirt."

She folds her arms over her chest and pouts. "Adults always say not today when they mean never."

Lucky for me I have the best excuse possible. I point outside. "You can't ride rollercoasters when it's raining."

"You can't?"

"Nope. It's too dangerous."

"But I want to go there! Piper's been there loads of times!" She sticks out her bottom lip and it quivers. Uh oh. Meltdown is impending.

I point to the calendar on the refrigerator. "Tell you what. Find a Saturday or Sunday when both your dad and I aren't working and we'll go to *Mermaid Mystical Gardens* then." I glare at Lucas. He better not shoot my idea down. "I know your dad is looking forward to it."

"I can't wait to ride the *Atlantis Adventure*," he says.

I smile. "Lame. *Kraken's Drop* is more my style."

"What's *Kraken's Drop*?" Natalia asks.

"It's…" Ah, shit. It's a drop tower ride that she's probably too short for. "Shoot. I just remembered. It's under construction."

"Nice save," Lucas whispers to me and I pretend to scratch my nose with my middle finger. He bursts into laughter.

"What's funny?" Natalia glances back and forth between the two of us. "Are you bonding?"

"You know what bonding is?" I ask.

She shrugs. "Piper's mom said Dad and you need to bond if you want this marriage to work."

Lucas scowls. "She said those words to you?"

"Well, um…"

"You were eavesdropping," he concludes.

Natalia's nose scrunches. "She was talking real loud."

He pulls on her ponytail. "What am I going to do with you, cupcake?"

She bats her eyelashes at him. "Watch *The Princess Diaries* with me?"

"How many times have you seen that movie?"

"Dad," she whines. "You can never watch *The Princess Diaries* too many times."

"Are we talking about the first movie or the second one?" I ask.

"Duh. The first movie. It's way better."

"I don't know. I think I prefer the second one."

"We have both. We can watch them both."

"And then compare which one is the best?"

"Dad." Natalia pulls on Lucas's sleeve. "Can we? Can we? Please!"

"The game is on today."

Natalia rolls her eyes. "There's always a game on."

He pretends to think about it. "I guess I can watch the game on my tablet while you watch the movie."

"Yes!" She throws her arms around him.

I stand. "I'll make the popcorn."

"I'll get the movie." Natalia darts to the living room and dumps a box of DVDs on the floor.

I find a bag of popcorn and throw it in the microwave. While it pops, Lucas sidles up to me.

"Thank you," he whispers.

"For what?"

"Spending your free day watching movies with my daughter. You must have better things to do."

Better things to do than spend the day with him and his daughter? I don't think so. There's no other way I want to spend my time.

I can hardly tell him how I'm falling in love with him and his daughter, though. He made himself perfectly clear. This marriage is a professional agreement. Nothing more. He wouldn't even have sex with me until I agreed it wouldn't change our relationship.

"What else am I going to do with this raging hangover? Go cliff diving?"

"You dive off cliffs?" He shakes his head. "Why am I not surprised?"

I don't actually dive off cliffs but the microwave dings before I have a chance to correct his assumption.

I pour the popcorn into a bowl and gather drinks for everyone. When I enter the living room, Natalia is curled up on the sofa next to her dad under a blanket. I hand her the bowl before settling in a chair.

"What are you doing?"

"Watching a movie."

"No, silly. Why are you sitting over there?" She pats the empty space next to her. "Come sit with me."

I hesitate for a second. I shouldn't get too used to having these two in my life. It'll only hurt more when I'm no longer needed.

But, let's face it, I'm not exactly known for making good decisions.

I move to the sofa and cuddle under the blanket with Natalia. Lucas murmurs *thanks.*

He doesn't need to thank me for loving his daughter. She's easy to love. I'm afraid her dad is easy to love, too.

Chapter 24

Family – can include a fake wife if you want it to

LUCAS

I check the time on my phone. "Natalia, come on! We're going to be late."

Natalia bounds down the stairs. "I'm ready."

"Have fun!" Chloe waves from the sofa where she's working on her laptop and watching some reality television show on failed bars while mumbling how stupid the bar owners are.

Natalia frowns. "You're not coming?"

"It's a family day, squirt."

"And you're family."

Pain washes over Chloe's face before she blinks and it disappears. "I'm not really family."

Natalia stomps her foot. "Yes, you are!"

Chloe motions to me. "You have your dad with you. You two will have a great time."

"But I want you to come."

Chloe blows out a breath. "Sweetie, I don't belong there."

"Yes, you do," I say because I'm done watching Chloe suffer. I don't want her ever to be in pain. But family brings up a bunch of pain for her. Her mother really did a number on her.

Chloe's gaze shoots to mine. "Excuse me?"

"You're my wife. You belong with us."

I'm lying but the words don't feel untrue. I want them to be true. I want Chloe to be my wife. My real wife. I want to spend every Sunday the way we did this past week – cuddled up together under a blanket watching a movie together.

I'm falling for this beautiful wildcat who hates the word beautiful and doesn't realize her own value. I run a hand down my beard.

My feelings don't matter. I can't take a risk on Chloe. She showed her true colors when she ran after we spent the night together. I can't chance another woman abandoning my daughter. Natalia has to be my priority.

But I can't stand the pain on her face. As long as Chloe is living in this house as my wife, I will shield her from anything that hurts her.

"Okay. Fine." Chloe slams her laptop shut and Natalia cheers. "But I'm not participating in any sports."

Natalia tugs her toward the door. "Don't be silly. Parents don't do the sports. The kids do."

Chloe draws the back of her hand over her brow. "Phew."

"Let's go." I herd them out the door.

"Someone's Mr. Punctual," Chloe mutters under her breath.

"Nothing wrong with being on time."

I hold Natalia's free hand and together we walk to the sports park with Natalia in between us, jabbering the whole time. Chloe listens and responds to my daughter's nonsense. She never loses patience. Even when Natalia asks the same question several times, hoping for a different outcome.

Holly would have told her to shut up by now. I don't know what I was thinking. I should have divorced Holly the first time she dumped Natalia at my parents' house.

"Piper!" Natalia waves at her friend and yanks on my hand. I don't let her go. There are too many people here. I don't want my daughter getting lost in the crowd.

I accompany her to the check-in where the counselors from her summer camp wait.

"Hi, Miss Madison!"

The teacher glances up from her clipboard. "Hey, Natalia. You're participating in the high jump, long jump, and hurdles today."

"I did high jump and long jump in high school," Chloe says.

"Because you got kicked off the cheerleading squad," Madison says.

"Technically, I was never on the cheerleading squad, so I couldn't get kicked off." Chloe winks. "How are you, Maddy? I haven't seen you in forever."

"Probably because I fall asleep by nine from exhaustion."

"Hello, Madison. I'm Lucas," I introduce myself. "Natalia's my daughter, and Chloe is my wife."

"No need to introduce yourself. Everyone on the island knows you married the wild child."

Chloe cringes when Madison says wild child and I squeeze her shoulder. She smiles at me and my heart seizes. Yep. I'm falling for this woman.

"Can I go now?" Natalia asks.

Madison hands her a number to pin on her shirt. "High jump is first. You can line up with the other kids who are competing there." She points to a line of children.

"Thanks, Maddy," Chloe says. "Let's get a drink and catch up."

Madison snorts. "Not if the drink involves you shooting moonshine all night and then dancing on the bar."

Chloe rolls her eyes. "That happened one time." She glances up at me. "I don't have the best balance."

I chuckle. "You don't say." I throw my arm around her. "Come on. Let's get Natalia sorted and then find a place to watch from the bleachers."

Natalia sprints to the high jump line where her friend Piper is waiting.

"Good luck," I tell her.

"Kick a—" Chloe cuts herself off. "Kick butt."

Natalia waves but in the next second we're forgotten as she begins talking to Piper. I lead Chloe away.

She bites her lip as she stares at Natalia. "Is she going to be okay? Some of those kids were half a foot taller than her. They have an unfair advantage."

"She'll be fine. They're high-jumping not joining fight club."

"Okay," she agrees but continues to nibble on her lip.

I know how to distract her. "Let's get a drink and a snack." We join the line. "What do you want to drink?"

"She'll have a *Five Fathoms Summer Ale,*" a woman behind us says.

Chloe giggles. "Hey, Lana. Have you met my husband?"

Lana rakes her gaze up and down me. "I have not met this long drink of water."

Chloe places a hand on my waist. It's possessive. A move I usually find irritating. A move that had me grinding my teeth when Holly did it. But with Chloe, I don't mind. I want everyone to know she belongs to me.

Except she doesn't.

"This is Lana, the mayor," Chloe explains.

I hold out my hand. "Lucas."

"Officer Fellows. I expect I'll need a police officer very soon."

"Lana," Chloe growls. "Do not take advantage of my husband."

She bats her eyelashes. "It's not taking advantage if he enjoys it."

"Don't make me phone your husband Ronald."

"Oh, poo. You're no fun."

I bark out a laugh. I bet no one's ever told Chloe she's not fun before considering the woman is all about enjoying life.

"Next!"

I use the excuse of being next to order to get away from Lana.

"What kind of beer do you have?"

Chloe elbows me. "What kind of beer do they have? What do you think?" She motions to the cans lined up on the counter. "*Five Fathoms Brewing* of course."

"I've never had a *Five Fathoms* beer."

"You've never had beer from your wife's brewery?" Lana asks. So much for getting away from the mayor.

"What do you recommend?" I ask Chloe.

"We'll have two cans of *Five Fathoms Summer Ale,* a bag of popcorn, and a bag of peanuts," she orders without hesitation.

"I'm not hungry."

"Good. Since the food is for me and I don't share."

I pay for our purchases while Chloe carries our tray toward the bleachers. We claim an empty spot in front of the high jump. The kids are lined up but haven't begun yet.

"Go, Natalia! You're a winner!" Chloe shouts before sitting down next to me. "I hope you don't mind but I plan to scream and shout for Natalia the entire time."

"Why would I mind my wife supporting my daughter?"

Happiness sparks in her light green eyes. "Good answer, hubby of mine."

"Did you like the beer?" Lana asks as she sits next to me.

"Lana. Don't push him."

"He's your husband. He should support you. Trust me. I know. I've had three husbands."

I pop the can of beer open and take a sip. I'm prepared to lie and say the beer is good regardless of how it tastes but it is good. I don't know why I'm surprised. Everything Chloe does, she does well.

"What do you think?" Lana asks.

"I think my wife's beer is excellent."

Chloe rolls her eyes. "I didn't brew it."

I wrap my arm around her shoulders and draw her near. "No, but you own the brewery."

"I don't own the brewery."

"Well, I never," Lana declares.

"What?" I ask.

"Never thought I'd live to see the day when Chloe Summers was modest about anything."

"It isn't Summers anymore," Chloe points out.

"Never thought Chloe would get married either. She must love you something fierce."

Chloe gasps. I glance down at her but she won't meet my gaze. Is Lana right? Is Chloe in love with me? If she's in love with me, why did she run the morning after we had sex?

Damn. This woman is a mystery I want to spend the rest of my life unraveling. Layer by layer.

Lana stands. "I'll let you two lovebirds enjoy your day."

"I can be modest," Chloe shouts after her. "Ignore her. She's crazy."

"Isn't she the mayor? I think that makes her my boss."

She scrunches her nose up. "Lana's more in charge of the tourist stuff not the serve and protect stuff."

I chuckle. "Serve and protect stuff?"

She waves her hand. "It's what police are supposed to do – serve and protect."

"Except I spend more time dealing with sheep than I do serving or protecting anyone on Smuggler's Hideaway."

Her light dims. "Do you not enjoy living on the island? Are you thinking of moving away?"

I probably should. I should hightail my ass far away from this island and Chloe before I get in too deep with this woman who has flight risk tattooed on her forehead.

"Dad! Dad!" Natalia shouts. "Watch me! I'm next."

But I won't go anywhere. My daughter has never been this happy before. And, if I'm being honest with myself, I'm pretty happy with my current situation as well.

But how long will it be before Chloe runs again?

Chapter 25

Mama bear – what Chloe turns into when bullying is involved

CHLOE

Addy knocks on the door of the storeroom. "Hey, boss."

I roll my eyes. "You don't need to call me boss." It drives me nuts when people call me boss. I'm Chloe. Nothing more. Nothing less.

She grins. "I know."

"What's up?"

"Your phone's been ringing nonstop."

"Which is why I left it in my office. I need to finish this annual inventory today."

"I shouldn't have looked but it's your stepdaughter. She's trying to reach you."

My brow wrinkles. "Natalia?"

"You have another stepdaughter you haven't told me about?"

There's a lot I haven't told my waitress. Starting with how my marriage to Lucas is fake with a capital F and ending with *I'm in so much trouble because I'm falling for my fake husband.*

Addy hands me the phone. "Please answer it before the ringing sound drives me bonkers."

"It's not ring—" The phone rings and cuts me off.

Addy giggles before waving and shutting the door behind her as she leaves.

"What's up, Natalia?"

"Can you come pick me up?"

I check the time on the phone. "You're supposed to be at summer camp for another two hours."

"I need someone to pick me up now."

I know what those words mean. I've said them to my mom enough times in my life. She's in trouble. But first things first.

"Are you hurt?"

"No."

"Are you sure?"

"I promise I'm not hurt. Can you come, please?"

"On my way." Because I will never not come when Natalia calls. Even after my agreement with Lucas ends, she can call me and I'll come running. Natalia deserves nothing less.

I get to my feet and throw my clipboard on the floor before rushing out the backdoor to my bike. I pedal as fast as I can to the summer camp.

Lucas's squad car isn't parked on the street at the entrance when I arrive. Of course, he could have walked. The police station isn't too far from here.

I drop my bike on the lawn and hightail it to the office building. I burst inside to discover Natalia and Piper sitting on chairs in the hallway.

"You came!" Natalia shouts and rushes to me.

I wrap my arms around her and haul her near. "Of course, I came." I release her to search for any injuries. "You aren't hurt?"

"I'm not hurt. Promise."

"What happened?"

Madison steps into the hallway. "Mrs. Fellows."

Now is not the time, but a jolt of excitement charges through me at her use of my married name. I'd love to be a Fellows. Shedding the last name of Summers would get rid of another reminder of dear old mom.

But Maddy using my married name is not a good sign. She's well and pissed. Crap on a mermaid cracker.

"I'll be right back," I tell Natalia before following Madison into an office.

Another girl and her mother are waiting there for us.

"No!" I know a set-up when I see one. Don't ask me how. I blame Sophia and her obsession with Flynn.

"What's the matter, Mrs. Fellows?" Madison asks.

"We are not having a discussion about whatever this is with one child present. Either all children involved are present or this meeting isn't happening."

Madison scowls. Probably because she knows I'm right. "Sheila, can you wait in the hallway?"

Sheila? Why does the name sound familiar?

The girl fists her hands and glares at me as she stomps toward the door. Now I remember. Sheila is the little girl who bullied Natalia.

Her mom jumps to her feet and blocks the door. "No, the girl who hit my daughter is out there. She won't be safe."

I snort. "Safe? Your daughter has been bullying my Natalia all summer long."

"My daughter is not a bully."

I cross my arms over my chest. "Said by all mothers of bullies all over the world."

"Ladies!" Madison shouts. "This isn't helping."

"As if she's a lady," the woman mutters under her breath.

I might not be a lady but – contrary to public opinion – I know when to keep my mouth shut.

"Mrs. Wurth," Madison growls.

"What? It's the truth."

I don't know this woman and she's being a bitch to me. No wonder her daughter's a bully.

"This is not constructive," Madison says.

"Let's bring the children in so we can hear both sides of the story," I suggest.

"There's no reason to hear both sides! Your brat child punched my daughter! She should be punished. She should be kicked out of summer camp."

The door flies open and August rushes in. "Sorry, I'm late."

She has perfect timing if you ask me. Otherwise, I'd be the one in the hallway in trouble for punching Mrs. Wurth.

"Mrs. Hill," Madison greets.

"Uh oh. We're in trouble. Maddy's using our surnames," August whispers, and I bite my tongue before I laugh. "What happened?"

"Your daughter is a liar!" Mrs. Wurth screeches at her.

August growls. "Do not call Piper a liar."

"She lied and said my precious Sheila pushed Natalia. Sheila would never push anyone."

"Quiet down everyone," Madison orders. "Before I phone the police."

"Go ahead," I say. "Contact the police."

August giggles. "Words no one ever thought Chloe Summers would say."

"The police are biased since this one," Mrs. Wurth points to me, "is married to an officer."

I inhale a deep breath and remind myself I can't get away with smacking her even though I am married to a cop.

"Please get your finger out of my face," I manage to say.

She wags her finger in my face. "Why? Does this bother you? Can't handle it, can you?"

"Geez. I wonder where her daughter learned to be a bully from." August taps her cheek.

Madison forces her way in between me and Mrs. Wurth. "Why don't we all sit down and stop using the word bully?"

I frown. "Why? Because Sheila's been a bully all summer and you didn't do anything about it?"

Guilt flashes on her face. And I am done. I do not put up with bullies. And I definitely don't put up with summer camps that don't do anything about bullies.

"Okay. This is what's going to happen," I begin.

"Who do you think you are?" Mrs. Wurth asks.

"I'm the person who's going to have her daughter report every single incident of bullying by your daughter until the camp does something about it. I'm the person who's going to phone every other parent in the school and make sure they know your daughter is a bully. I'm the person who's going to speak to the school district about their bullying policy. Need I go on?"

Mrs. Wurth shrinks away. "No."

I address Madison. "Are we done here?"

"I can't allow Natalia to return to summer camp."

"Fine." Summer camp is over in two days anyway. We'll figure out some way to keep Natalia occupied until school starts next week.

"I'm sorry, Chloe." Madison wrings her hands together. "I know how you feel about bullying after what…"

I hold up my hand before she can mention my past. "Apology accepted but this stops now."

"Understood."

I grasp August's hand. "Let's go."

She squeezes my hand. "I'm with you, Chloe."

I open the door and Natalia rushes to me. I drop August's hand to hug her.

"I'm sorry, Clo-Clo." She bursts into tears. "I didn't mean to get you in trouble."

"It's okay." I sway her from side to side until she stops crying. I lean back and wipe the tears from her eyes. "This is not your fault. You hear me? Not your fault."

I wait for her to nod before releasing her.

"Okay. Let's get out of here."

I wave to August who's holding a distraught Piper. "I'll call you."

"You can send Natalia to my house for the next two days. I work at home anyway."

I thank her before exiting the building with Natalia. I frown when I notice Lucas still isn't here.

"Where's your dad?"

"Um…"

"Out with it."

"I didn't phone my dad."

Fear rocks through me. Will Lucas be mad at me for handling this situation? For not reaching out to him?

Shit. Shit. Shit.

If Lucas says Natalia is *his* daughter again and I have no say in her upbringing, it'll break my heart. I can't handle it.

"Y-y-you need to call your dad," I stutter.

"But Clo-Clo," she whines.

"No, I'm sorry, Natalia. But he needs to know. He should have been here for this meeting."

Lucas didn't get a chance to have his say and now he's going to lose his mind. And Natalia will not be the one he's angry with.

I only hope he doesn't end our marriage now. I'm not ready to let him go.

I'm afraid I never will be.

Shit.

Chapter 26

Pull your head out of your ass – when you change the deal

LUCAS

"Did your kid learn your right hook from you?" Weston asks.

"What the hell are you talking about?"

"You didn't hear? Natalia got in trouble for punching some bully at summer camp. She didn't phone you?"

I dig out my phone as it begins to ring.

"Someone's in trouble," Weston sings as he backs out of the locker room.

"Natalia. What happened?" I answer.

"It's not a big deal."

Which means it is a big deal. But her punching a kid is not a discussion I want to have on the phone.

"Where are you?"

"Chloe's taking me home."

"Chloe's there?"

"Don't be mad at her. I phoned her instead of you but when she found out I hadn't contacted you, she made me call you."

"I'm not mad at Chloe." I'm relieved she showed up for my daughter again. Despite how I was an asshole and told her Natalia's my daughter to deal with.

"Good because Chloe's worried."

She doesn't need to worry because things between us are about to change. I'm pulling my head out of my ass.

"I'll meet you at home."

By the time I make it home, Chloe's bike is in front of the garage. Good. They're here. I open the door and Natalia rushes to me.

"I'm sorry, Daddy. I know I shouldn't have punched Sheila but she pushed me. She always pushes me. And says nasty things about me. She calls me a bastard."

Chloe growls. "You didn't tell me about the name calling."

Natalia shrugs and her cheeks darken.

Chloe drops to her knees in front of my daughter. "Listen to me. No matter what names people call you, you don't take it on." She places a hand over Natalia's heart. "You listen to who you are in here. No one else can say who you are. Only you."

"Okay, Clo-Clo."

Chloe tweaks her nose before standing. "I'll let you and your dad talk."

I tag her hand before she can escape. "I want you here."

"Are you sure?"

"You're my wife. Of course, I'm sure."

I usher everyone into the living room. "What happened?"

Chloe opens her mouth to speak but I place a finger over her lip. "Not you. Natalia. What happened with Sheila this time?"

"She pushed me. I was first in line for lunch but she pushed me so she could be first." She pauses.

"And what did you do?"

"I punched her in the stomach."

"Punching is wrong."

"I know! But what was I supposed to do?" She throws her arms in the air with a huff. "Sheila's always pushing kids and saying nasty things but the teachers never do anything about it."

"Do the teachers know about it?"

"They do. Trust me. They do," Chloe mutters.

"And what happened at this parent meeting?" I ask.

"Chloe yelled a lot," Natalia says.

I cock an eyebrow at Chloe. Her cheeks burn but she nods. "I had things to say."

I stand and offer her my hand. "Chloe and I need to discuss what happened."

"Don't be mad at her, Dad. She was standing up for me."

I ruffle her hair as I pass. "Don't worry. I'm not mad."

I lead Chloe upstairs to my bedroom.

"I'm sorry, Lucas," she says as soon as the door is shut behind us. "I didn't know Natalia didn't phone you. I thought she did and you were running late. And I shouldn't have yelled when I got there. But Maddy wasn't doing anything about Sheila bullying Natalia and she *was* bullying her. Bullying her. I can't... Not bullying...My mom..."

She bursts into tears and I wrap my arms around her.

"Don't cry, wildcat. Your tears destroy me."

My heart aches for her. Today's incident brought up all the shit of the past with her mother.

I want to hunt down her mother and give her a piece of my mind. I usually work hard to not be intimidating when I'm in uniform since a police officer who towers over you can be frightening. But I want to frighten the hell out of Chloe's mom.

"I'm sorry."

Chloe leans back to meet my gaze. "Why are you sorry? You didn't do anything wrong. You're perfect."

I wipe the tears from her face. "I did, though. I yelled at you when you gave Chloe permission to sleep over at her friend's house when I should have been thankful to you for helping out. Being a parent to Natalia wasn't part of our deal."

"But—"

"Which is why our deal is changing," I say and cut her off.

Her jaw drops open. "Our deal is changing? You're kicking me out? I really am sorry. I…"

I slam my mouth to hers to stop her babbling. Her lips are salty from her tears. I growl. Chloe should never cry again because of her mother. And I will make sure of it.

I pull back. "From now on, you're not my wife in name only. This marriage is no longer fake."

Her green eyes cloud with confusion. "I don't know what's happening. Did I fall asleep doing inventory? Did the whole school incident not happen? I hope no one writes on my face with a Sharpie while I'm sleeping. I better not be snoring."

I chuckle. My wildcat never ceases to amuse me. "You're awake. And no one has written on your face with a Sharpie, but thanks for the idea."

She rolls her eyes. "As if Mr. Law and Order would ever write on my face without permission."

I'd do a lot of things she wouldn't expect of me. Including binding her to my bed naked and not letting her go until we're both satisfied and unable to walk.

"What do you say, wildcat? You want to make a go of this relationship?"

"I don't understand. You've made it clear you don't want a relationship."

Because I was afraid before. Afraid Chloe would abandon us. But she wouldn't. This woman would kill to protect my daughter. She's the one I need in my life. I can't let her go.

"What's changed?"

I'm falling in love with my wife is what's changed but Chloe's not ready to hear those words. She'd flee the house faster than Natalia can disappear when it's her turn to do the dishes.

But I'm not letting Chloe run again. She's staying.

"I was afraid to expose Natalia to my dating," I lie. "But since you're living here and Natalia is used to you, there's no sense in worrying about it."

"Try again."

"What?"

Chloe leans close to my face. "Try. Again. You're lying."

"I'm not lying."

"You shouldn't lie to someone who's a master at lying."

I frown. Chloe's a master liar? This doesn't bode well.

"I can't tell you the number of times I told my mom I had to go to Sophia's because we had a school project we were working on. Lucky for me, Lily always backed me up."

I growl. "I hate your mother."

"And you haven't met her yet. I bet she'd try to seduce you."

I rear back. "Seduce me? Her daughter is my wife."

She shrugs. "I doubt your status as her son-in-law would stop her. I can't count the number of judges she seduced back in my pageantry days." She shivers. "Mom did whatever was necessary to ensure she won."

I brush her hair from her face. "But it wasn't her winning. It was you."

She laughs. "You really don't understand my mom. Everything I won was her win. Did you know she stole all of my trophies and ribbons when she left? Even the ones for track and field despite ordering me not to participate?"

I place my hands on her cheeks. "I'm sorry for all you went through. I wish I could take all of the pain away."

"But you can't. Trust me. Even Paisley's evil genius can't erase the pain."

"Your friends stood by you through all of it."

She smiles. "And then we founded a business together so they can never get rid of me."

"Wildcat, they wouldn't get rid of you without the brewery."

She shrugs and glances away.

"Another layer peeled away," I mutter. "What do you say, wildcat? You want to make this fake marriage into a real relationship?"

She bites her lip as she studies me. I drop all of my walls and allow her to witness how much I want her. How much I want this. How desperate I am for her.

"Should we make some ground rules?"

I frown. "What ground rules?"

"One, I'm keeping my house in case things go belly up. And, two, I still get to be friends with Natalia whether we're involved or not."

I thread my hand through her hair and tug until her neck is exposed to me.

"One, you can keep your house but things aren't going belly up. And, two, you can always be friends with Natalia because you'll be her stepmother."

"Don't jump the—"

I smash my lips on hers. I'm done discussing this. She agreed. We'll work on the details later. Hopefully, once she's attached to me so tight, she can't let go.

She moans and I thrust my tongue into her mouth. I'm desperate to taste her untamed flavor again. She wraps her legs around me and I whirl around to pin her to the wall.

My cock presses against my zipper. I'm ready to explode and we're both still fully dressed. Lucky for me, we don't need to get naked to get some satisfaction.

I sneak my hand between us and snap Chloe's jeans open.

"Are you guys fighting?" Natalia shouts.

I rip my mouth from Chloe's and lean my forehead against her shoulder while I catch my breath.

"We're not fighting!" Chloe hollers.

"Good! Because I'm hungry."

Chloe laughs and I pull back to watch. Her face is full of happiness. She's beautiful. And one of these days she's going to not cringe when I tell her how beautiful she is.

But not right now. Right now, I need to feed my wife and daughter.

Chapter 27

First date – especially anxiety inducing when it's with your 'fake' husband

CHLOE

I stare at myself in the mirror. "This is a bad idea. What was I thinking? Who goes to a beginner surfing lesson as a first date?"

"Is it a first date if you're married?" Paisley asks. I glare at her through the phone. We're FaceTiming since I'm at home trying on bikinis for my date with Lucas. "Sorry. I didn't mean…"

"Why do you think this is a bad idea?" Sophia asks. "He told you to plan the date."

"Which is romantic," Maya adds.

"Seriously? Is there anything you don't think is romantic?" The woman needs to get her head out of a book and start living her life. Being pen pals with a soldier doesn't count.

"It's a fun idea," Nova says before Maya can respond.

"I want pictures," Sophia adds.

I roll my eyes. "As if the four of you aren't planning to hide in the dunes and spy on us the whole time."

Paisley clears her throat. "I wasn't planning on hiding."

"Aha!" I point at the phone. "You're going to crash my date."

"It's not crashing if we merely observe," Paisley says.

"I for one can't wait to see Lucas in swimming trunks." Maya wiggles her eyebrows.

I return my attention to the mirror. "Maybe I should wear a one-piece. I must have a speedo somewhere."

Sophia growls. "You are not wearing a one-piece."

I motion to my body. "But a bikini? On a first date?"

"He's seen you naked. He's not going to be put off by you wearing a bikini," she reminds me.

"He'll probably be fighting a hard-on the entire time," Nova adds.

This idea has promise. Lucas turned on but unable to do anything about it. Teasing I can't get in trouble for.

"Huh. Maybe this is a good idea after all."

Lucas added a no sex rule to our agreement after Natalia almost walked in on us. I told him we could lock the door but he's afraid his daughter is going to figure out what we're doing. I don't know what his problem is. Parents have sex.

"Is he still sticking to the no sex rule?" Sophia asks.

"Yes." I groan. "Kissing is okay but no touching and no naked body parts."

"Technically, you don't have to be naked to have sex," Paisley points out.

"I know. I tried to get him to stick his hand down my pants but he wouldn't." I ended up in the shower taking care of business because I was about to explode otherwise.

"Maybe you should wear dresses," Maya suggests. "In historical romances, they lift the skirts and away they go with no one the wiser."

"I don't know. I think her tiny bikini and the water will work as well," Sophia says.

"Is my bikini tiny? Should I wear another one?" I rush for the closet.

"You've tried on all of your bikinis. This is the best one," Nova says. "Go have fun."

Lucas knocks on my door. "You ready, Chloe?"

I grab my cover-up – an extra-large t-shirt with the words *I stop for seals* on it – and slip it on before opening the door. "Ready."

I bound down the stairs and he groans.

"What's wrong? You don't want to learn to surf after all?"

He adjusts himself in his swim trunks. "I want to learn to surf but I don't know how I'm going to survive being around you with those long creamy legs of yours exposed the entire time."

I smirk. A surfing lesson was a good idea after all. "Just wait until we get in the water and I remove my t-shirt."

"You're cruel."

He snatches my hand and leads me out of the house to his truck. "We need to go now before I forget why I insisted on the no sex rule."

"I've already forgotten why you insisted."

He presses me against the side of the truck and thrusts his hard cock against my stomach. "You drive me crazy."

I glide my hands up his arms until I reach his shoulders. "Right back at ya, hubby of mine." I push up on my toes until our faces are level with each other. "What are you going to do about it?"

He grunts before wrapping an arm around my waist and dragging me close until we smash together. His lips meet mine and he shoves his tongue into my mouth. *Yes*. I've yearned for his taste on my lips all day. There's nothing better. Not even the tastiest beer can compete.

His fingers dig into my ass and I squirm against him for some much needed friction.

He wrenches his mouth from mine. "We can't do this outside."

I sigh. Thwarted again. "Shall we get to our lesson?"

He helps me into the truck and we're off. The beach where the surfing lessons happen is about halfway between Smuggler's Rest and Rogue's Landing. But it's still less than fifteen minutes. Nothing is far away on Smuggler's Hideaway.

We park and I notice Sophia's car. When we walk to the beach, I spot my girlfriends sitting on a blanket in the dunes. They brought a bucket of beer and snacks. I'm glad my dating life is entertainment for them.

I ignore them. I don't want Lucas to realize my friends are here. This is supposed to be our first date. Not a group activity.

We reach the hut to check in and I nearly groan when I realize who it is. Miles. I went to high school with him. He thinks he's funny. I don't find him amusing.

"Well, well, well, who do we have here?" he asks.

"Hi, Miles. This is Lucas."

Miles grins at Lucas as he offers him his hand. "Nice to meet the man who tamed the wild child."

Lucas growls. "My wife did not need taming."

Goosebumps erupt whenever Lucas growls *my wife*. I've never enjoyed a man who's possessive before but with him it's different. Everything's different with him.

"Alrighty then." Miles cringes before shaking out his hand.

"You can't break the hand of every person on Smuggler's Hideaway who calls me a wild child."

He winks. "I can try."

"Serve and protect, Mr. Straitlaced."

He steps close. "I already proved I'm not straitlaced. Maybe you need a refresher."

I grin. "I totally need a refresher."

He slaps my ass and steps away. "Wildcat, don't get us in trouble before the lesson begins."

"I didn't start it."

Miles clears his throat. "Go ahead and find a board and join the rest of the group."

There are five men already waiting by surfboards. I find a free board while Lucas glares at all of the men. He frowns when he notices the spot next to me is occupied. He prowls to the man.

"I want to be next to my wife," he grumbles at the man who immediately crumbles and scurries away.

"Be nice to everyone," I hiss at him.

"I'm not being nice to any man who eye fucks you."

"No one is eye fucking anyone."

"Wrong."

"Okay!" Miles claps his hands. "Let's get started. We're going to learn how to paddle, pop up on the board, and other necessary movements on the sand before we try them in the water. Everyone lay down on their board."

I whip off my t-shirt.

"What are you doing?" Lucas growls.

"I'm not getting my t-shirt dirty," I say as I stuff it in my bag.

"Do you want everyone to eye fuck you?"

"Just you, hubby."

His eyes flare, and I bite my bottom lip. He groans. "Wildcat."

"Lay down on your board and we'll practice how to pop up," Miles says.

I lay down on my board and Lucas follows suit. Several of the other students glance our way and he hurls glares and snarls their way.

I throw sand at him. "Stop being an animal."

"No one should stare at my wife's ass."

"What are you going to do when we travel to Europe and I go topless?"

He growls. "You are not going topless."

Nova rushes toward us. "I have a picnic set up in a romantic spot for you."

Sophia chases after her. "You're cheating!"

"He's probably uncomfortable with a hard-on pressed against the surfboard anyway," Paisley says as she joins them.

Maya is right behind her. She gives me a thumbs-up.

"Hard-on?" Lucas sputters.

Paisley's brow furrows. "Do you not have a hard-on?"

"Is that Paisley the Perpetual Know-It-All?" Miles asks.

Paisley whirls on him. "Please refrain from using childish nicknames."

He holds up his hands. "Sorry. It's what my brother, Eli, calls you."

"Yes, well, I have some childish nicknames for Eli, which I won't use because I am not a child."

I stand up to confront my friends and fist my hands on my hips. "I'm trying to have a date here."

Lucas lifts my arms before dressing me in his t-shirt. "I can't take you anywhere."

"I am not going in the water with this t-shirt on. I'll drown with how big it is."

He grasps my hand before picking up my bag. "Good. Because we're leaving."

"There are no refunds," Miles hollers after us.

"We'll reschedule."

"When I can have a private lesson with my wife," Lucas adds as he drags me away. My friends follow.

"Who had less than fifteen minutes?" Sophia asks.

I glare at her. "It's bad enough you were spying on us. Did you have to make bets, too?"

"I didn't bet," Maya says. "But I did prepare a picnic for you." She motions to where a blanket is set up between the dunes with a picnic basket.

"Maya the romantic strikes again."

"Do you want to have a picnic?" Lucas asks.

I tap my chin and pretend to consider it. "I don't know. A picnic with a hot police officer who's wearing a pair of board shorts and nothing else?"

He grins. "Picnic it is. Thank you, Maya."

She blushes and ducks her chin. "Welcome," she whispers.

We reach the blanket and I motion for my friends to go away. They bitch and complain, but they do leave eventually.

Lucas helps me to sit before sitting across from me. "I'm sorry."

"Sorry for what?" I narrow my eyes on him. "Did you sweat in this t-shirt before you put it on me?" I lift up my arm to sniff the armpits.

He chuckles. "No, I'm sorry I ruined our first date."

"You didn't ruin our first date."

"I yelled at all the men for eye-fucking you."

I smile. "I know. It was sexy."

"You're not mad we're not doing the activity you had planned?"

I shrug. "As long as there's beer in the basket, I'm good."

"You're amazing."

I toss my hair. "Thank you."

"No." He shackles my wrists. "Don't blow me off. You're amazing. Someone should tell you how amazing you are every day."

My heart catches in my throat. I would love him to be the one telling me I'm amazing every day. "Are you signing up for the job?"

"Maybe," he whispers. "Maybe."

His head descends and his lips meet mine. Another thing I want to experience every day. His lips on mine. His heat surrounding me. Me wearing his t-shirt.

Chapter 28

Beautiful – a word Chloe will stop hating if Lucas has anything to do with it

LUCAS

By the time we arrive home from our picnic, my cock is painfully hard and my balls ache. Chloe eating and drinking beer with a bikini on was sexy as fuck. I'm ready to bury myself deep inside her and not come up for air until I'm satisfied. Although, I have a feeling I will always want more with Chloe.

A note is taped to the front door. I snatch it.

I kidnapped Natalia. You may have her back in the morning. Go enjoy yourselves. Wink. Wink. Nudge. Nudge.

I hold up the note. "Who writes wink wink nudge nudge?"

"The note is signed Sophia."

He scowls. "I don't appreciate your friends kidnapping my daughter."

"We'll go get her." She starts for the car but I capture her wrist to stop her.

"Are you serious?"

"Of course. If you're uncomfortable with Sophia and Flynn babysitting Natalia for the night, we'll pick her up and do a movie night."

Damn. She is serious. Chloe would give up a night of guaranteed sex to go get my daughter. And here I thought I couldn't get any more turned on.

I tug on her wrist until she's plastered against me. "I trust Sophia to babysit Natalia. Correction. I trust Flynn to watch Natalia *and* Sophia."

The pulse in her neck flutters. "You do?" she breathes out.

"I do. But it begs the question…" I trail off to kiss her neck.

She tilts her head to provide me with better access. "W-w-what question?"

"What are we going to do with ourselves without my daughter in the house?"

Her fingers dig into my shoulders. "Are you lifting the no sex rule?"

I glide my finger down her neck and between her breasts before whispering in her ear, "If you want to."

"If I want to?"

I bite her earlobe. "Say yes."

"Yes," she hisses. "A bajillion times, yes."

I chuckle. "Bajillion?"

"We'll have Paisley explain a bajillion to us tomorrow. We're busy tonight."

I lift her up and she circles my waist with her legs. My cock presses against my shorts in a bid to get to where it wants.

I open the door and carry her inside. I make sure to lock the door behind us before carrying her upstairs and to my bedroom where she belongs. Where she's always belonged. I was a fool to fight this attraction before but I've learned the error of my ways.

I lay her on the bed and cover her with my body.

"You've been driving me wild all evening."

"Right back at ya. I thought your calves were the sexiest part of your body but after spending dinner studying your chest, I'm not as sure." She draws a finger over my tattoo. "This ink is particularly sexy."

I chuckle. "My calves?"

She drags her fingernails lightly up and down my back. I love the feel of her hands on my body. But it's my turn to touch her. To drive her crazy with need. To give her pleasure until she's blinded by it.

I get to my knees. "As much as I love you wearing my clothes, this t-shirt has got to go."

She lifts her arms and I whip the t-shirt off. I groan when her tiny red bikini is revealed. Her breasts are barely covered by the top.

"I fucking love this bikini." I trace my finger along the edge of the material. "But you are never wearing it in public again."

She wraps her legs around my waist and rubs her core against my cock. "You're cute if you think you can tell me what I can and cannot wear."

I unwind her legs and pin her thighs to the bed with my hands. "I'm in charge here."

She glares at me in response but she can't fool me. I felt her full body shiver.

"Don't move."

I wait until she nods to stand. I dig around in my dresser until I find what I want. I lift the handcuffs in the air. "You okay with these?"

She nods.

"I need the words."

"Yes, Mr. Law and Order, please handcuff me to your bed while I'm naked and have your wicked way with me."

I grin. "Your wish is my command."

I cuff her hands separately to the slats in my headboard. I stand and observe my handiwork. She's my captive. I can do to her what I want.

Because she trusts me. Chloe doesn't trust many people outside of her small circle. But she trusts me. She shared things with me about her mother her friends don't know. This woman is mine. I'm keeping her.

"Spread your legs."

She widens her legs and I kneel in between them. I glide my fingers up and down her legs. Goosebumps follow in my wake.

She pulls on the handcuffs. "Are you going to touch me tonight?"

I freeze. "Am I not touching you now?" I slide my palm along the outside of her leg.

"You're not touching the good parts."

I circle a freckle on her thigh. "Is this not the good part? Your creamy skin. I love how soft it is."

She groans. "You're going to drive me crazy, aren't you?"

I wink. "Maybe."

She doesn't back down. My Chloe never backs down. She doesn't let life beat her up. She falls down. She gets back up. "I guess I'll have to wear this bikini more often then. Mowing the lawn. Cleaning the house. Rid—"

I pinch her nipple and she gasps. "Yes."

I pull on the string between her breasts and the material falls away to reveal her creamy breasts. I knead and massage them until she's squirming beneath me. Only then do I take one into my mouth. I lick and suck until her nipple is a hard point. Then, I switch breasts.

"So pretty," I murmur. Her breasts are red from my beard and her nipples are pointing straight at me. She arches her back but I don't accept her invitation. It's time to move on.

I toy with the edge of her bikini bottoms. She plants her feet on the bed and lifts herself in offering to me.

"Such a needy little thing."

"I need you inside me."

I love it when a woman tells me what she wants.

I drag a finger along the gusset of her bikini bottoms. "You want my fingers?"

She shakes her head.

"My mouth?"

She shakes her head.

"My cock?"

"Yes. I want your cock."

My cock twitches in response. It's on board with this plan. It's done with the teasing. It's done with the sole pleasure it gets being my hand. It wants Chloe's warm, wet pussy surrounding it.

I tug on the strings of her bottoms on her hips and the material falls open. I shove it out of my way and thrust two fingers into her.

"Yes," she hisses.

"You're soaking for me."

She opens her mouth to answer but I press the heel of my hand against her clit and she moans instead.

"I love hearing the little moans and sighs you make for me, but I'm going to make you scream. Make you shout my name."

"Okay," she breathes out.

I start pumping my fingers into her. She lifts her hips to meet me.

"After you come on my fingers, I'll give you my cock."

I watch her face as she seeks her pleasure. Her cheeks are flushed and sweat dots her brow. She's beautiful. And she should know it. She should know there's nothing wrong with beauty.

"You're beautiful, wildcat."

"Not beautiful."

"But you are. The most beautiful woman I've ever seen."

She opens her eyes to glare at me. "Not beautiful."

"Don't let your mother take this away from you. She's taken enough from you."

Her jaw clenches. "Not. Beautiful."

I pause with my fingers buried deep inside of her. She mewls in protest.

"Accept you're beautiful and I'll let you come."

"You're an asshole."

I brush the hair off of her forehead and cup her cheek. "Wildcat, you need to know you're beautiful. Inside and out."

"I don't want to be beautiful. All Mom cared about was beauty. She tortured me."

I draw a finger along her lips. "I know, wildcat. But you're letting your mother control your life even though she's no longer a part of it."

Her nostrils flare. "I am not."

"Okay, beautiful."

A vein pulses in her forehead. "I am not beautiful."

"You are beautiful and you know it. But you're afraid of the word because it reminds you of your mom. Take the word back, wildcat. Be the strong woman I know you are and take it the fuck back."

Her lips purse but the vein in her forehead is no longer pulsing.

"Say it with me, I am beautiful."

I press the palm of my hand against her clit. "Say it and I'll make you come so hard you'll see stars."

"You're not supposed to use sex to get your way."

"Wildcat, you're naked and handcuffed to my bed. I already got my way."

Her eyes soften and I nip her bottom lip. "Say it with me. I am beautiful."

"I am…"

I thrust into her a few times as a reward and her breath hitches.

"Come on, wildcat. You can do this. You can do anything you want to. You're the strongest woman I know. The smartest woman I know. The kindest woman I know."

"Iambeautiful," she mutters.

I slam my lips down on hers and pump my fingers in her. I breathe in her ocean flavor as my tongue explores her mouth. When her walls flutter around my fingers, I lift my gaze to watch.

Her head falls back and her mouth falls open. "Lucas."

"Come for me, beautiful. Come all over my fingers."

"Yes. Yes. Yes."

"Say my name when you come. I want my name on your lips when you climax."

"Lucas!" she shouts as her walls tighten around my fingers. I continue to thrust into her until her orgasm wanes. Until she's boneless on the bed. Only then do I remove my fingers and push my shorts down my legs.

I quickly don a condom.

"Now, it's my turn," I mutter as I hitch my cock at her entrance.

I thrust inside. Home. This woman is my home.

Chapter 29

Pancakes – the answer is always pancakes

CHLOE

I awake enveloped in Lucas's arms and snuggle closer to him. I have no desire to be anywhere else in the world but in the arms of the man I love.

The man I love? I don't love Lucas. I'm falling for him but I don't love him. Not yet.

Except, I have no desire to run away. Even after he forced me to admit I was beautiful last night. Usually, I punch a man when he's being pushy. But when Lucas opened the handcuffs, I threw myself at him.

Shit. It's official. I love Lucas.

"What has you thinking so hard this morning?" he asks in a scratchy morning voice I want to hear every morning for the rest of my life.

I can hardly admit I just realized I love him. He might be ready for a relationship but we haven't known each other long enough for love. Except I fell hard and fast.

He rolls over until he's looming above me. "You aren't considering running again, are you?"

"Nope."

He studies my face. "Really?"

I push up to give him a quick kiss. No tongue is allowed until I've had a chance to brush my teeth. "Really."

"Thank fuck. I'm not in the mood to chase you."

"You didn't chase me before."

"Before I was denying how much I want you in my life, wildcat."

"And now you're done denying it?"

He tweaks my nose. "I made it clear I was done denying myself when I told you this marriage is no longer fake."

"Good thing I'm not running then."

"Good. We've got better things to do." His gaze catches on my mouth and I bite my bottom lip. Screw the whole brushing the teeth rule.

He punches his hips forward until I feel his hard cock, hot and heavy against my stomach. And my stomach rumbles. Loudly.

I cover my face in embarrassment. "Ignore it."

"Nope. If my wildcat's hungry, she's getting food."

I start to pout but my stomach rumbles again.

Lucas frowns. "You didn't eat enough at our picnic last night."

"It's hard to concentrate on food when the man who kisses you each night before denying you sex is sitting before you with his chest on full display."

He chuckles as he bounds out of bed. He shackles my wrist to help me out, and I wince. He frowns as he studies the red marks on my skin.

"Shit. I didn't mean to hurt you."

"Pretty sure it was me hurting myself when I strained against the cuffs because you were driving me mad."

"Still. We won't use cuffs again."

I pout. "You won't tie me up again?"

He smirks. "I didn't say there wouldn't be any tying up in the future. In fact, I can't wait to tie your hands and your legs up."

"My hands and legs?" An image of me spreadeagle on the bed flashes in my mind and I moan.

His cock twitches. "You're tempting me, but these marks need to heal before I tie you up again."

I lick my lips. "I know some things we can do that won't hurt my wrists." I nod toward his cock.

He groans. "The first time you take me in your mouth won't be while your stomach is rumbling."

I place a hand over my stomach, which is indeed rumbling. "I guess you better feed me."

He helps me out of bed and urges me toward the bathroom. "Get ready while I make breakfast. Do you want pancakes or sausage and eggs?"

"Pancakes. The answer is always pancakes."

He chuckles. "I should have known my little sugar addict wants pancakes."

"I'm not addicted to sugar. I can stop eating it whenever I want to. But I don't want to." I spent the first eighteen years of my life being denied sweets and chocolate. I am never living without it again.

Lucas prowls toward me. "Stop."

"Stop what? Eating sugar? I just said I refuse to."

He palms my neck and places his forehead against mine. "Stop thinking about your mother."

I roll my eyes. "You're the one who brought her up last night. During sex, I might add."

He squeezes my neck. "Because I can't stand how you cringe whenever anyone says you're beautiful. You are beautiful. You should be able to hear the word without freaking out."

"I'm not freaking out now." Maybe a little bit but at least I didn't cringe.

He grins. "Because I fucked your hatred of the word right out of you."

I gasp. "You did not!"

"Are you certain? I can replay what happened for you."

Dang it. He called my bluff. "I thought you were going to make me breakfast."

He whirls me around and prods me toward the bathroom with a pat on my ass. "Do your thing. I'll have breakfast waiting for you."

Gotta love a man who knows how to pick his battles. And, yes, this is the man I love. I clutch my chest. I can't believe I fell in love with my fake husband.

I force the panic away. I'm not going to worry about the future. I'm going to enjoy the moment. The future will have to sort itself out.

When I enter the kitchen a few minutes later, Lucas is at the stove flipping pancakes without a shirt on. I study his broad back as his muscles bunch with his actions. I want to feel those muscles move beneath my hands.

Hey. Wait a minute. I can.

I join him at the stove and wrap my arms around him. He glances over his shoulder and smiles at me. This man's smile is dangerous.

I'd do crazy things to see his smile every single morning for the rest of my life. Such as marry him to protect his daughter and then fall in love with him. It's official. I *have* done crazy things.

"There's coffee in the pot."

I kiss his shoulder before releasing him. "Do you need a top up?"

I fiddle with the coffees and pour us some orange juice while he finishes up the pancakes. He slides a stack of three pancakes on my plate.

"Don't worry. There's more."

I giggle. "Smart man."

"I have a daughter. I know to keep the pancakes coming."

I glance at Natalia's empty spot at the table. "Is it crazy to say I miss her?"

Lucas squeezes my hand. "You love her. Of course, you miss her."

"She's very loveable."

The door bangs open and Natalia bursts inside. "I'm home!"

"Speak of the devil," Lucas mutters before standing to hug her. "Welcome home, cupcake. Did you have fun?"

"We had a ball! We played flashlight tag and cornhole and then we made smores on the firepit outside. Can we get a firepit?"

"I'll think about it," Lucas says.

She turns to me. "What do you think, Clo-Clo?"

"I'll speak to your father." I wink.

"Is there coffee?" Sophia says as she trudges inside and drops several bags at the bottom of the stairs. "Please say there's coffee."

I point to the counter. "Didn't you have coffee at home?"

"We did," Flynn says as he enters. "But it wasn't enough."

Sophia glares at him. "You're the one who decided we should build a fort and watch movies."

He shrugs. "I thought she'd fall asleep."

"Instead, she sang every song in the movie."

I giggle. "No one asked you to babysit. You kidnapped Natalia."

Sophia salutes me with her coffee mug. "Was it worth it?" She waggles her eyebrows.

I feel my cheeks heat.

"Awesome," she mutters.

"What's awesome?" Natalia asks.

"Me," I say. "I'm awesome."

She gets a gleam in her eye and I worry I've just made a mistake. A big mistake.

"Awesome stepmoms take their stepdaughters to *Mermaid Mystical Gardens.*"

Sophia bursts into laughter. "You walked right into that."

I raise my eyebrow at Lucas. "What do you think?"

"It is Sunday and you did promise her we'd go to the amusement park the next time we both had off on the weekend."

"YES!" Natalia squeals at the top of her lungs. "I'm going to ride the rollercoaster first. Or maybe the spinning teacup. I need to phone Piper. She'll know what rides are the best."

She sprints to the stairs but screeches to a halt and spins around before running to me. She throws her arms around me.

"Thank you, Clo-Clo. You're the best stepmom in the world."

She rushes away before I have the chance to thank her or tell her she's the best stepdaughter in the world.

"Welp. I'm out of here before I get roped into joining you." Sophia tags Flynn's hand and leads him toward the door.

"You love the rollercoasters," I holler after her.

She lifts her mug in response. "I'll bring this back later."

Lucas chuckles.

"What?"

"Have you ever taken a kid to an amusement park before?"

I shake my head.

"This is going to be fun."

I don't know what he means, but it will be fun. I get to spend the entire day with my two favorite people at one of my favorite places on earth.

What could possibly go wrong?

Chapter 30

Revelation – not necessarily a surprise if you suspected it all along

Lucas

"Piper says we need to do the bumper cars, too," Natalia says as I park at *Mermaid Mystical Gardens*.

She hasn't stopped talking since we started driving. Granted, the drive isn't long but still. My daughter is a chatterbox.

"The bumper cars are called *Bubble Bash*," Chloe explains as we walk toward the entrance. "The cars are designed to resemble submarines and the floor looks like the ocean."

"Cool! More ocean stuff. I like the mermaid stuff the best."

"Me, too."

We reach the booth to pay and Chloe tries to elbow me out of the way. "I should pay. It was my idea."

"But Natalia is my daughter and you're my wife. I'm paying."

"Let him pay!"

I glance behind Chloe to wave at the mayor. "Hi, Lana."

"Hi, tall drink of water."

"He's not water," Natalia says. "He's my dad."

Chloe giggles. "It's a compliment. It means your dad is handsome."

"According to the counselors at summer camp, my dad is the most handsome of the dads."

"They're right," Chloe whispers.

"What did you say?" Lana asks. "I didn't hear you."

I shove a ticket into Chloe's hands. "This is yours."

She scowls. It's adorable. "I wanted to pay."

"Too bad, wildcat."

"Can you at least lie and say I can pay next time?"

"Nope." I grasp my daughter's hand and lead her toward the turnstiles.

"It's common courtesy to lie," Chloe grumbles.

She's cute. "You have a strange definition of courtesy."

"Whatever," she mumbles and scans her ticket before pushing through the turnstile.

"All right, cupcake," I say once we're inside the park. "Where to first?"

She points to a teacup ride but instead of teacups, there are clamshells and sea urchins.

"*Triton's Twister.* Good choice." Chloe takes her hand and they skip toward the ride and get in line.

"What about me?" I ask.

"You can hold my purse," Chloe says.

"You're not carrying a purse."

"I want a drink, Daddy. A coke!"

"You're not having a coke. You can have a lemonade."

Chloe bats her eyelashes at me. "Am I allowed to have a coke?"

I shake my head. "I'll get the drinks. You enjoy your ride."

The attendant opens the gate and kids rush to find a clamshell or sea urchin. Chloe looks around before entering through the exit and securing a clamshell. I'd say she's a bad influence on my daughter but Natalia is smiling and laughing.

Lights flash and the song *Under the Sea* plays as the clamshells and sea urchins start to spin around. The kids scream in excitement but loudest of them all is Chloe. Her arm holds Natalia close to her as they both scream in delight.

Damn, I love that woman.

The revelation doesn't surprise me. I think I've been in love with Chloe since she whisked Natalia away for a day of pampering when she got her first period. The way she loves my daughter is a sight to behold.

She's fiercely protective. I wish I could have witnessed her sticking up for Natalia when she got in trouble for punching another kid. I bet she was magnificent. After how Holly treated her own flesh and blood, finding Chloe is a miracle.

But I don't love Chloe merely because she loves my daughter. I'd love her even if Natalia wasn't in the picture. She's smart and funny and has more layers to her than an onion. I've enjoyed peeling those layers away these past weeks. Discovering things about Chloe she keeps secret from the world.

And she's sexy as hell. Sex with Chloe is the best I've ever had. The way she trusts me in the bedroom is so fucking arousing, it's addicting.

Chloe isn't ready for words of love from me. Getting her to agree to take a chance on me was hard enough. But I can be patient. I'm not going anywhere.

The ride ends and Chloe helps a wobbly Natalia out of the clam shell and to the exit. I wave them over to where I'm standing.

"I want to go on the rollercoaster next!"

Chloe giggles. "You're still dizzy from *Triton's Twister*."

"I thought you wanted a drink," I say before Natalia can argue with Chloe and steer the two of them toward a refreshment stand.

"Now, can I go on the rollercoaster?" Natalia asks once we have our drinks.

"You need to finish your drink first."

"I can finish the drink in line."

"She has a point. The line for the *Sea Serpent Coaster* is thirty minutes now." Chloe waves her phone at me.

"You downloaded the app for *Mermaid Mystical Gardens*?"

She rolls her eyes. "No, silly. I already had it."

"But this amusement park is for children."

She giggles. "You're cute. Naïve. But cute."

"Do I get to at least ride the rollercoaster with you?" I ask Natalia as we begin to walk toward the coaster.

"I'll ride by myself. You two can ride together," Chloe offers.

We join the line. Natalia bounces up and down.

"Do you have to go to the bathroom?" I ask although I'm pretty sure I know the answer.

"I can wait."

Chloe feigns a grimace. "I can't. Do you want to go with me?" She hands me her soda. "Hold our place in line."

When they've been gone ten minutes, I start to get worried. I'm reaching for my phone to call Chloe when I hear her.

"My husband is holding our spot."

"I don't care. I've been waiting here for fifteen minutes with no one to hold my spot. Maybe I need to go to the bathroom," a woman says. I crane my neck but I can't see either one of them.

"Go ahead," Chloe tells her. "I'll hold your spot."

"It was hypothetical."

"You don't need to pee?"

"No."

"Then, why are you making a fuss? Come on, Natalia."

"But you're cutting in the line."

"What's your email address?" Chloe asks.

"My email address? What do you need my email for?"

"I'll send you some information about what cutting a line is. Because this ain't it."

People laugh before Natalia and Chloe come into view.

"What took you so long?" I ask.

"The line for the restroom is nearly as long as this line." Chloe winks at Natalia.

The line moves and it's our turn to board the rollercoaster. Chloe rushes toward the back. She helps Natalia into the last car of the rollercoaster before sitting in the spot in front of her. I join Natalia and make certain she's strapped in.

Chloe glances back at us. "Who's excited?"

I frown at the empty seat beside her. We should have another child. One of each. A boy and a girl. I bet I can convince Chloe to have my baby.

The ride starts and we begin a slow ascent to the highest point of the rollercoaster.

"I don't feel very good," Natalia whines.

I groan. "Please don't throw up."

"Deep breaths through your nose and count backward from one hundred by fives," Chloe suggests.

"100. 95. 90. 85. 80."

We reach the peak and fly down the other side.

"Whoo hoo!" Chloe shouts and Natalia joins her. Her nausea completely forgotten.

By the time the ride ends a minute later, Natalia is smiling and laughing.

The ride stops and I help to unbuckle Natalia while Chloe jumps out and lifts her out of her spot.

"Awesome! Can we go again? I didn't get sick."

"Maybe later," I say to put her off.

Chloe leads her to the exit and I trail behind them.

"What next?" Chloe asks when we're back on the main thoroughfare.

Natalia doesn't get a chance to answer before my phone rings. I dig my phone out of my pocket and scowl at the caller ID. Holly. Why the hell is she calling?

"I need to take this."

Chloe shoos me away. "We'll wait by the bench over there where we can see the mermaids."

"What do you want?" I answer the phone when I'm certain I'm out of hearing range.

"Where are you?" Holly asks.

"What business is it of yours?"

"I'm at your house. I want to see my daughter."

"You can't show up and demand to see Natalia."

"I'm not leaving until I see her."

"I'll be there in fifteen minutes." I hang up before she has a chance to gloat.

"What's wrong?" Chloe asks when I return to them.

"There's an emergency. I need to go."

I hold my breath as I wait for her to yell at me or demand to know what's important.

"I hope no one's injured. Go. Do your sexy cop thing. I'll ring Sophia to pick us up when we're finished."

She's not bitching or complaining?

"Will you be okay on your own?"

She grins. "We'll be better than okay. We don't have to worry about you slowing us down."

She's serious. She's not hurt or offended or mad. She's perfectly okay with me leaving to handle an emergency. Although, if she knew what the emergency was, she might feel differently. I'll get rid of Holly before she arrives back home.

I hug Natalia. "Be good and listen to Chloe."

"I will, Dad."

I kiss Chloe. "Thank you."

She pushes me away. "Go do your serve and protect gig. I got this covered."

I open my mouth to say I love you but manage to snap it shut before I blurt the words out. Wrong place. Wrong time.

"See you at home," I holler before hurrying out of the park.

Knowing Chloe and Natalia will soon follow me has me rushing home to deal with my ex. Holly is no longer my family. My real family is at the amusement park. And the two shall not meet.

I won't allow my ex to hurt my family. I don't care what I have to do.

Chapter 31

Cookies – the solution to all your problems

CHLOE

Natalia moans and I tighten my arm around her. "Do you need to stop?"

"Wanna go home."

Guilt swamps me. I never should have let Natalia talk me into letting her ride the *Sea Serpent Coaster* again. Her getting sick all over my shoes is my penance for trying to get her to love me the way I love her.

"We'll be there soon," Lily says from the driver's seat.

"Thank you for picking us up."

"No need to thank me. I'm always there if you need me." She turns around to smile at Natalia. "The same goes for you, kiddo. If you need anything, ring me."

"Thank you, Mrs. Milton."

"You can call me Lily, Grandma Lily, or Grandma."

Lily is the best. Forcing Sophia to be my best friend in kindergarten was the best idea I ever had.

"Huh. Strange," she says when we turn into our street.

"What is it?"

"There's an unknown car in your driveway."

I peer out of the window and notice there's a car in the driveway as well as Lucas's truck. Shouldn't he be at the station handling whatever emergency came up?

Lily pulls to a stop in front of the house. "I'll wait here for a few minutes."

"There's no need. Everything will be fine."

"Nevertheless."

I don't argue. Lily will do what she wants to anyway. Besides, I need to get Natalia inside. She has more color in her face but she's still cluctching her stomach and moaning.

I slide out of the car and gather Natalia in my arms. "Almost there, kiddo."

"I'm sorry, Clo-Clo."

"Nothing to be sorry about. It's not your fault you got sick."

I open the door with my shoulder as I carry Natalia inside. It's a good thing I have experience carrying six grocery bags into the house at one time or I'd probably drop her.

I freeze at the entrance when I realize Lucas is standing in the living room facing off with a woman.

"Chloe, Natalia?" Lucas asks. "What are you doing here?"

"Natalia wasn't feeling well."

He rushes forward to take Natalia from my arms but she slaps away his hands. "Mom?"

She squirms to get down and I steady her. "Mom! It is you! You're here!" She darts across the room and throws herself at her mom.

Holly purses her lips as she pats Natalia's back. "Hello, Natalia."

"I'm excited you came to visit. You're going to love Smuggler's Hideaway," Natalia rattles on. Her sickness completely forgotten. "They have mermaids and seals and there's the beach. The water is cold but it's okay once you get used to it. We can build sand castles together."

Holly steps away from Natalia. "We can discuss what we'll do together after I speak to your father. Now run along with your nanny while the grownups speak."

Natalia's shoulders slump forward in disappointment. Her bottom lip trembles. "But Mom…"

Holly scowls. "No begging. It's unbecoming."

Unbecoming? Is this woman serious? Her daughter, who she hasn't seen for a year, is excited to see her and she brushes her off. And then gets annoyed when Natalia is disappointed. Nuh uh. Not on my watch.

I march forward and place a hand on Natalia's shoulder.

"Surely, you and Lucas can speak later. After you've spent some time with your daughter. Natalia would love to show you her room and the medals she received at sport's day last week."

Holly sniffs. "The nanny is in no position to speak to me about what I should do."

"Good thing I'm not the nanny then."

She waves a dismissive hand at me. "Lucas's little plaything then. It makes no difference. You have no right to be here."

Lucas growls and wraps an arm around my waist. "This is my wife."

Holly rolls her eyes. "I'm your wife. Not this…"

Her gaze rakes up and down my body. I'm wearing a pair of cut-off jean shorts and a t-shirt with a mermaid on it. Whereas she's dressed to impress. Her sheath dress is molded to her skin and her high heels are at least three inches tall.

I can understand why Lucas was attracted to her. She's gorgeous with long blonde hair and bright blue eyes. She also has the curves I've always dreamed of.

"This is my wife," Lucas grumbles. "You're my ex."

I glance down at Natalia who seems to be shrinking into herself. She should be the center of attention now. Not her mother.

"Why don't you two continue this discussion and Natalia and I will go elsewhere to watch a movie?"

"You're not taking my daughter anywhere!" Holly shouts.

"Okay. We'll stay here and you two can go get a coffee. I recommend *Pirates Pastries*. You should try Blackbeard's revenge cookies. They are to die for."

Her nose wrinkles. "Cookies? I don't eat sugar."

Of course, she doesn't. I bet she goes to the gym, too. She probably thinks having a gorgeous body and face means she can be a bitch.

She's in for a rude awakening. I've been down this road before. I know how rotten a person can be on the inside despite their outward appearance.

"I'm trying to be nice," I warn her.

"Nice? You stole my husband," she screeches.

Natalia's bottom lip trembles. She's on the verge of tears. She shouldn't be a witness to this discussion.

"I'm begging you to take the adult discussion elsewhere. Somewhere Natalia isn't."

"Begging?" She snorts. "I bet you do a lot of begging."

"Enough," Lucas grumbles. "You don't disrespect my wife."

"You never minded it when people disrespected me," Holly claims.

"Maybe because your idea of disrespect was when a waitress didn't rush to fulfill every one of your needs."

"It's literally her job."

"I'm done." I'm not allowing Natalia to hear any more venom come out of her mother's mouth. "Let's go, Natalia."

I lead her to the door. I don't have a plan. All I know is I won't allow Natalia to witness this scene any longer. I should have left the second I realized her mom was here. But I thought Holly would at least pretend to be excited to see the daughter she hasn't seen in a year. My bad.

Holly runs ahead of us and bars the door. "You're not going anywhere."

"We'll go out the back door." I whirl around.

Lucas growls before stepping beside me. "Touch her and you and I are going to have even bigger problems than we already have."

I glance over my shoulder and notice Holly has her hand lifted as if to slap me. Unfortunately, I'm familiar with how a woman who's about to lose her shit and slap me appears.

There's a knock on the door before it opens and Weston enters.

"Hey, bro. Heard you might need an assist."

Lucas nods to me and his daughter. "Can you get them out of here?"

I frown. Get us out of here? Not his ex?

He kisses my forehead. "I need to discuss some things with Holly. I'll come get you when she's gone."

"Gone? I'm not leaving!" Holly shouts.

"My mom is waiting outside with the car," Weston says.

I wrap an arm around Natalia's shoulders. "You wanna go to Grandma Lily's house?"

"Can we watch a movie?"

"Yep. I bet she'll bake us some cookies if we ask real nice."

Weston accompanies us to the door.

"Bye, Mom." Natalia waves. "We'll do some fun stuff when I get home from Grandma's house."

Holly forces a smile on her face. "We will, baby. We will."

Not if I can help it, they won't. This woman is toxic. I don't want her anywhere near Natalia.

Lily rushes forward. "Natalia! Are you ready to come to my house? We can bake some cookies."

"What kind of cookies?" she asks.

"What kind is your favorite? We can stop at the grocery store for ingredients."

Weston shuts the door behind us. "I could go for some cookies."

Lily frowns at him. "You can have cookies when you give me grandchildren."

He grins. "I'd break all the women's hearts in Smuggler's Hideaway if I chose to settle down with one woman."

"My son." Lily shakes her head. "He won't know what hit him when he falls in love."

"Good thing I'm not planning to fall in love."

"What kind of cookies should we bake?" I ask Natalia once we're in Lily's car driving toward her house. "I love chocolate chip."

"Oatmeal raisin are my favorite."

"Gross. Raisins shouldn't be in cookies."

She giggles and I sag in relief. She's not traumatized by what happened with her mom and dad. Still, I'm going to keep an eye on her. I won't let this girl suffer the way I did because of a crappy mom. Not on my watch.

Chapter 32

Try – should involve some form of effort but usually doesn't when an ex is involved

LUCAS

I watch as Natalia and Chloe leave the house. I'm torn. I want to be with them. I want them with me. But I don't want my daughter or my wife anywhere near Holly.

The contrast between Holly and Chloe couldn't be more obvious. Holly stands here dressed in clothes meant for a country club I could never afford. And don't want to. Meanwhile Chloe's beautiful as ever in her jean shorts and t-shirt.

Their appearances aren't the only difference between my past and my future. Holly is a complete bitch who didn't bother pretending to want to spend time with her daughter. Whereas Chloe fought to keep Natalia safe.

"Finally." Holly draws a sharpened nail down my arm. "We're alone."

I retreat a few steps. "Don't touch me."

She flutters her eyelashes. "You used to enjoy it when I touched you."

"When I was twenty-three and didn't know better."

She flicks her hair over her shoulder. If the move was supposed to be sexy, she missed her mark. Her bleached hair stiff from all the product she uses, doesn't appeal to me. I much prefer auburn hair wild from being loose in the wind.

"Don't lie. We've had sex since then."

Hardly. Once Natalia was born and Holly showed her true colors, my interest in sex with her vanished.

"We're divorced, Holly," I say instead of reminding her of how I turned down her advances again and again. No one enjoys being turned down but Holly was humiliated. I tried to soften the blow but there's a limit to how nice I can be when I awake to a woman I don't desire with her mouth around my cock.

"I want to try again."

Try? I snort. She didn't try the first time.

"Not interested."

She bites her bottom lip. "I bet I can change your mind."

She'd lose that bet. "I'm married, Holly, and I'm no cheater."

"Are you insinuating I'm a cheater?"

"No need to insinuate. I walked in on you sucking his dick, remember?" I sure as hell wish I didn't remember. The sight should have pushed me to divorce her. But I didn't want Natalia growing up without a mother.

Since I've heard Chloe's story, I realize how wrong I was. Having a mother who's absent and has no interest in your life is worse than not having a mother.

She rolls her eyes. "I don't know why it's such a big deal."

"I told you this a million times already. Cheating is wrong. And I can't be with a cheater."

"I promise I won't cheat again. It was a mistake. I've learned my lesson."

She learned her lesson? She walked away and never looked back. She's barely contacted her daughter in the past two years since she left. And she hasn't seen her daughter in the past year. None of her actions indicate she's learned anything.

"I'm married."

She dismisses my words with a wave of her hand. "Do you seriously expect me to believe you're actually married again? You claimed you'd never marry again. And yet you suddenly have a wife the minute I ask for custody."

"Ask for custody? You claimed you'd sue me for sole custody. I'm not letting you steal my daughter away."

"Exactly." She nods. "Which is why you came up with this whole fake wife thing. It's okay. I won't tell anyone. But there's no need to continue the charade."

"The charade?"

She points to next door. "Your *wife* has a house next door. If you were married, she wouldn't still have her house."

"How do you know the house next door is from her?"

She smirks. "You're not the only one who can do some investigating."

Shit. I fell into her trap.

"Whether Chloe rents the house next door or not is immaterial. We're married and I'm not letting you steal my daughter."

She jabs me in the chest with her finger. "She's *our* daughter. I'm the one who carried her for nine months. I'm the one who had to get a boob job because my breasts sagged from nursing her."

I remove her hand from my chest. "You carried her for nine months, but there's more to being a mother than giving birth. You never paid Natalia any attention. You didn't play with her. You ignored her in her crib. When she began school, you didn't participate in any of the school activities. You didn't bake for the bake sales. You didn't go to her school plays. Need I go on?"

"That's all in the past now. I'm a changed woman."

"Which is why you cringed when Natalia hugged you? Why you're here having this argument with me instead of spending time with the daughter you haven't seen in a year?"

"It's not a big deal. I can spend time with her later. I'm not going anywhere."

I inhale a deep breath and pray for calm. If Holly wants to see Natalia, I have to give her the chance to be in her daughter's life. No matter how much it hurts me. It's not about me. It's about my daughter.

"Are you moving to Smuggler's Hideaway?"

"I can hardly be with you if I don't live in the same place as you."

"You are not hearing me, Holly. I'm married. I'm not leaving Chloe to be with you."

"And you're not hearing me. I know your marriage is a sham."

Panic grasps me for a second. She knows I married Chloe to keep Natalia safe? I force those thoughts away. It doesn't matter why I married Chloe. We're together now and I'm not letting her go.

"Chloe is my wife. Our marriage is not a sham."

She crosses her arms over her chest. The action pushes her breasts together but I look away. I'm not interested in any other woman than Chloe. Especially not a scheming woman who will do anything to get her way.

"You are forcing my hand."

"I'm not forcing anything. I'm telling you the truth."

"We'll see what the judge thinks of your 'marriage'."

"You're suing me for custody of Natalia?"

"I'm not going to let you win."

I growl. "Natalia is not a prize. She's our daughter."

"She's also a girl. A girl should live with her mother."

I snort. "Which is why you prepared her for getting her first period."

She shrugs. "I wasn't here. I couldn't prepare her."

"You weren't here because you didn't want to be. You didn't fight me when I asked for full custody of Natalia when we divorced."

"Yes, well. Things have changed."

I narrow my eyes. "Things have changed? I beg to differ. You obviously don't have any more interest in Natalia than you did when we were married."

I wanted to tear her from limb to limb when she brushed off Natalia. Lucky for me, Chloe stepped in or I would be in jail for assault now. My wife was fucking magnificent. I want to be with her and not having this ridiculous conversation with Holly. I'm not changing my mind on a damn thing anyway.

"Like I said. Things have changed."

What things could have possibly changed? What could...

I shake my head when I realize what's happening. I should have realized this before. Holly wants money.

"You want child support. What happened to your latest boyfriend? Did he kick you out?"

She winces. Gotcha! She's after money.

"You can't use child support to support your lavish lifestyle. Child support is for the child."

"A child needs somewhere to live, food to eat. If I use the money for rent and food, it's not wrong."

She doesn't even bother denying she wants custody for the child support money. This has nothing to do with wanting to spend time with her daughter.

"You can get a job and earn money for rent and food."

"I don't have time to work."

"What the hell are you doing with your time that prevents you from having time to work?"

"You wouldn't understand."

In other words, she's doing what she's always done. Getting manicures and pedicures on a weekly basis. Going to lunch with her girlfriends who have rich husbands. And shopping for clothes she can't afford.

"You disgust me."

"Whatever. There's no judge in this world who won't give a mother custody of her daughter."

I cross my arms over my chest and glare down at her. "You're wrong. Natalia is part of a loving family. A judge isn't going to rip her away from it."

"Did you forget your marriage is a sham?"

"My marriage is not a sham. Chloe is my wife." And she always will be. I'm not letting her go.

"I'll prove otherwise and the judge will agree with me having custody."

"Bring it on, Holly. I will fight you every step of the way."

She purses her lips. "You want Natalia to be a witness to us fighting?"

Of course, I don't want Natalia to watch her parents fight over her in court. But I'm not letting Holly steal my daughter because she needs money.

"She'll witness a dad fighting for his daughter. There's nothing wrong there."

She sighs. "I don't know why you have to be this difficult."

I'm the one being difficult? Holly always has been delusional.

I motion to the door. "It's time for you to leave."

"You're not going to let me stay here?"

Completely and utterly delusional. "My family lives here. You are not a part of my family."

She stomps her foot but I'm not letting her throw a temper tantrum. I herd her toward the door.

"Have your lawyer contact my lawyer," I say before shutting the door in her face.

I wait until she gets into her rental car and drives off before I dig out my phone and dial Chloe. I need to be with my family after experiencing that shit show.

Chapter 33

Staying – harder than running away. Scarier, too.

CHLOE

"Is everything okay?" I ask Lucas once we're finally in bed.

We're both exhausted and ready for sleep. It took a while for Natalia to settle down. She was understandably upset when we returned home and her mom was gone. And hadn't bothered to leave a message for her. But I need to know what happened between Lucas and Holly.

He climbs into bed next to me. "I wish I didn't have to tell you this, but I do."

I roll over to face him. "Tell me what?"

"Holly is suing for custody of Natalia."

That bitch doesn't deserve to have a daughter. With more control than I thought possible, I keep my tone calm. "We knew this was bound to happen. It's why we got married in the first place."

He cringes. "About our marriage…"

"What is it?"

He cups my chin. "Holly knows our marriage started out fake."

I gasp. "But how? My friends and family know but they wouldn't tell anyone. Small towns love to gossip but they know how to keep secrets, too."

He brushes the hair off of my forehead. "I don't know how she knows. I don't know what she knows. But I wouldn't be surprised if she claims we got married to fool the judge into granting me custody."

My stomach dips. This is worse than I thought. I can't believe Holly knows.

"It's going to be okay." He wraps his arms around me and draws me near. I melt into his arms where I feel safe. The only place I've ever felt completely safe and accepted.

He kisses my hair. "Go to sleep. We'll talk to a lawyer this week and figure things out."

Within minutes, Lucas's breathing evens out. But I can't sleep.

Thoughts churn round and round in my mind. Would Lucas be better off if I weren't in the picture? Will it hurt his chances of keeping custody of Natalia if the judge finds out our marriage is fake?

Should I leave?

Should I stay?

When the first streams of daylight are visible through the window, I still don't have an answer. I think I know what I need to do, but I'm afraid.

I'm a coward. I don't want to lose what I've found with Lucas. My one safe place where the loneliness doesn't plague me. Where I can forget all about my past.

I crawl out of bed and dress quickly before sneaking out of the house and biking to the brewery. I'll have some privacy here since the place is still locked up tight.

I sit behind my desk and switch on my computer. Time to do some research. Fingers crossed I won't have to leave Lucas to secure Natalia's safe and happy future.

"I found her!" Sophia shouts. "She's in her office."

I lift my head off my desk and brush my hair out of my face. I must have fallen asleep.

"Do you have to be loud?"

"Don't yell at me for being loud. I wasn't the one who snuck out of my house and freaked my husband out."

"Lucas is freaked out? Why didn't he message me?"

I dig my phone out of my bag and notice it's on silent. I cringe when I see I have two missed calls from Lucas and one from Sophia. "Oops."

Sophia enters the room and sits in a chair across from me. "What's going on? Why did you sneak off this morning?"

Maya strolls into the room. "Maybe she was overwhelmed by her love for Lucas and ran."

I roll my eyes. "My life is not a romantic novel."

"It's pretty romantic, though," Nova says as she joins us.

Paisley pokes her head in the room. Great. The gang's all here. So much for having privacy this morning.

"Can we stop beating around the bush now?" Paisley asks. "I assume Chloe's here because Lucas's ex-wife arrived on the island yesterday and caused a scene."

"Chloe," Sophia tsks. "I thought you were done running from Lucas."

"I'm not running. I'm thinking."

"About what?"

Nova peers over my shoulder at my computer. "This isn't good."

I slam my laptop shut but I'm too late. She already saw my research.

"You're worried Lucas is going to lose custody of Natalia," she says.

"Of course, I'm worried. Lucas loves Natalia. He would be devastated to lose her."

Paisley taps her toes. "But this isn't why you're at the brewery before the office opens."

I duck my chin and study my fingernails. "Yes, it is."

Sophia glances back and forth between Paisley and me. "What's going on? And why does Paisley know?"

"I know because I know Chloe." Paisley clears her throat. "She's going to leave Lucas."

Nova sighs. "Really, Chloe. Why would you throw your happiness away?"

Maya frowns. "But you love him."

It's because I love him. I don't want him to have to choose between Natalia and me. He will always choose Natalia. Which is the only choice I'd accept anyway.

Sophia plants her hands on my desk and leans close to study my face. "She actually thinks she's doing the right thing."

"I knew I should have stopped at *Pirates Pastries* on my way here." Maya aims for the door. "If we're going to persuade Chloe to stay with Lucas, we need drinks. I'll make mimosas."

I rush after her. "You are not getting your hands on my bar."

Maya giggles. "But I got you out of your chair, didn't I?"

Sophia, Nova, Maya, and Paisley perch on the barstools while I gather champagne and orange juice to make mimosas.

"I'm first," Sophia declares. "Leaving Lucas is stupid."

Paisley frowns at her. "How is this a good argument?"

Sophia shrugs. "Chloe hates it when she does stupid stuff."

She's not wrong. But leaving Lucas isn't stupid.

"You love him," Maya says. "You should be together."

I shrug and pop open the champagne bottle.

Sophia slams her hands down on the bar. "Holy bootleggers in heaven! Chloe loves Lucas!"

"What are you talking about?" I hedge. I haven't told Lucas I love him yet. I'm not telling my friends first.

"Maya claimed you love Lucas several times now and you haven't contradicted her once."

Time to change the subject before I end up declaring my love for a man I can't have. "Whether I love Lucas or not doesn't matter."

Maya gasps. "How can it not matter? Love is the only thing that matters."

"You really need to stop reading romance novels."

"You can pry my romance novels from my cold, dead fingers."

"Don't tease Maya," Nova urges. "She loves romance. There's nothing wrong with a little fantasy now and again."

I salute her. "Yes, Ms. Sunshine."

"Being an optimist is not a negative personality trait no matter how much you make fun of me."

Ugh. Now, I'm being a bitch. "Sorry, Nova. I love your sunshiny personality." Just not right now.

I concentrate on mixing our drinks as I explain, "If Lucas has a better chance of winning a custody suit if I'm out of the picture, it's better if I leave him."

"This is ridiculous!" Sophia shouts. "You married him to give him a better chance of winning a custody suit."

"True. But we assumed his bitchy ex-wife wouldn't find out about our arrangement."

Her brow wrinkles. "She found out? How?"

I shrug. "I don't know. I trust every single person who knows the truth."

"I believe it's immaterial," Paisley says.

I pause pouring the champagne. "Explain."

"Your relationship is obviously real now. A judge will observe the two of you together and conclude the same. There's no reason to leave Lucas."

Is she right?

"Maybe," I mutter as I finish pouring the champagne and add the orange juice.

I set a glass in front of each woman but when I reach Nova she holds up a hand. "None for me, thanks."

"But you love mimosas."

"Not today. My tummy is acting funny."

Uh oh. Nova is a bit of a hypochondriac. She has her reasons, which is why we don't push her.

"More for me." I swipe her glass and replace it with one filled with pure orange juice.

Sophia lifts her glass in the air. "To Chloe making good choices!"

"To love!" Maya shouts.

I sip on my drink, but I don't think my friends will agree with my choices. Because despite what Paisley said, I can't chance Lucas losing Natalia. I don't want either one of them to suffer. I love them too much.

I would do anything for them. Including break my own heart.

Chapter 34

Love – is the answer. Just ask Maya.

LUCAS

"Chloe! Are you home?" I shout when I return home after work. "Are you okay?"

I bound up the stairs. Sophia messaged me to go check on Chloe. Since Chloe snuck out of the house this morning, I didn't hesitate to rush home after reading the message.

I peek in my bedroom, but it's empty. As is the connected bathroom. And the hallway bathroom. I enter the guest bedroom to discover Chloe packing her things.

"What the hell are you doing?"

She jumps and drops the clothes in her arms. "What are you doing home early?"

I point to the suitcases on her bed. "Are you leaving me? I fucking knew it. You're running scared."

"I'm not scared. I'm doing this for you."

I rear back. "For me? You're hurting me for me? If you cared about me, you wouldn't do this."

"I love you, Lucas. With all my heart. It's why I'm doing this."

Warmth spreads through me at her confession. Hell yeah. This woman I'm obsessed with loves me.

I prowl to her. "I love you, too, wildcat."

I reach for her but she bats my hands away.

"I'm still leaving."

My muscles tense. She's still leaving? "Why the hell are you leaving if we love each other?"

"I don't want you to lose Natalia."

The anger drains from my body and warmth replaces it. "This is about Natalia?"

"Of course, this is about Natalia. You can't lose custody of her. Holly can't have her. Your ex will destroy the light in your little girl's eyes and I won't have it."

Damn, I love this woman. She loves my little girl something fierce. It's everything I ever wanted for my daughter to have.

"You won't, have it?"

"Don't make fun of me. I know how it feels to be raised by a narcissistic mother. How it feels to wake up every morning wondering what kind of mood she'll be in. Will today be the day she lets you eat breakfast or will she lock you in the closet for asking for a bowl of cereal? Why do you think I don't want children? I can't become my mother."

I shackle her wrist before sitting on the bed and pulling her on my lap. "You aren't your mother."

Her brow wrinkles. "I know."

I cup her cheeks. "You said you're afraid of becoming your mother if you have children."

"Shit," she mutters and glances away.

"No." I pinch her chin and force her to meet my gaze. "No hiding from me. You can't tell me you're afraid to have children and then hide from me."

Her eyes narrow. There's my wildcat. "I said I don't want children. I didn't say I'm afraid to have them."

I grin. "You love children."

She scowls. "I didn't say I love children."

"Okay, I'll edit my statement. You love my daughter."

"Natalia's easy to love."

I chuckle. "She threw up on you on a rollercoaster yesterday."

She shrugs. "It happens. Ask me about the time Sophia drank six shots of moonshine before getting on the rollercoaster."

"Nice try, but you can't distract me."

"Distract you from what?"

I grin. This woman can amuse me even when we're having the most important discussion of my life.

"Chloe Fellows, you are not leaving me."

The sparkle in her eyes dies out. "I have to Lucas. I can't risk you losing Natalia. I would never forgive myself."

"I'm not going to lose custody of my daughter."

"But Holly knows our marriage is fake."

I growl. "Our marriage isn't fake."

"Correction. Holly knows our marriage started out as fake. She could use the information to persuade a judge to give her custody."

I tuck a strand of hair behind her ear. "I already spoke to a lawyer."

"You did? When? Why didn't you tell me?"

I pinch her nose. "Someone hasn't been answering her phone all day."

"Oh."

"There's only one attorney on Smuggler's Hideaway who handles custody cases. Apparently, he's been fielding calls all day from people on the island who want to testify about how our marriage is very much real. About how we're in love and can't keep our hands off each other."

She frowns. "Can't keep our hands off each other? Who said that?"

I smirk. "No one but it's true."

"You're serious? People have actually been contacting Mr. Ezra about us?"

"Yep. And Ezra says it doesn't matter anyway. Holly hasn't visited or contacted her daughter since we arrived on the island. It seems the local judge doesn't approve of mothers who don't show up at Family Sports Day."

"Makes sense. Judge Clara broke her foot doing the long jump on Family Sports Day. Since her parents weren't there because they were both working, she ended up going to the hospital with a teacher. She had to have surgery to put a pin in her ankle and her parents weren't there. I don't think she ever forgave them."

"Is there anyone on this island you don't know?"

She scrunches her nose as she pretends to consider my question. I tickle her ribs and she giggles as she tries to wiggle out of my arms.

"Stop it. This is a serious discussion."

I throw her on the bed and crawl on top of her. "The serious portion of the discussion is finished. The fun part is about to begin."

She strains at my shoulders. "But I haven't told you I'm staying."

I bite her bottom lip in punishment. "You're staying. I'm not letting you go."

"You can't order me around."

"I love you. You love me. You're my wife. You're not leaving."

"But I don't want children. You need to find a wife who will give Natalia brothers and sisters."

"I found my wife. It's you."

"But children?"

"We have Natalia. She's enough."

For now. I know I can convince Chloe to give me more children. She's afraid but I'll show her there's nothing to be afraid of. I'll show her each and every day she's nothing like her mother.

Once she realizes she isn't her mother, she'll agree to give me babies. She loves children. She's just afraid.

"Really?"

I kiss her nose. "Really."

She bites her bottom lip and mischief sparkles in her eyes. "I'd stay but all of my clothes are packed."

I glance around the room at her suitcases. "Good."

"I'm confused. You want me to move out? I guess we could date for a while. Although I'd miss sleeping with you at night."

I press my hard cock against her stomach. "You're not sleeping anywhere but with me."

"Are you deliberately being confusing? Why are you happy my bags are packed?"

"It makes it easier to move your clothes into my room."

She gasps. "Into your room?"

"Our room," I amend.

"Maybe we should slow things down. This is moving extremely fast."

"I know what I want and what I want is you, my wife, sleeping in my bedroom with me every night. Your bathroom shit spread all over the vanity in the bathroom."

"I'm not messy."

"Wildcat, I've seen the hallway bathroom. Yes, you are."

"Fine, I'm messy. How messy would you be after eighteen years in a house where you had to vacuum the carpet in one direction because otherwise your mother would lose her mind?"

I draw a finger down the vein on her forehead that started pulsing at the reminder of her mother. "I like your mess."

"You do?"

I nod. "Are we done talking now?" I grind my hard cock against her and her eyes flare.

"Yes," she hisses.

"Good, because I want to make love to my wife now."

"Your wife approves of this plan."

"Approves?" I pump my hips again. "Not excited?"

"Trust me. I'm excited." She wraps her legs around my hips. "Prove to me I made the right choice, hubby dearest."

"Gladly."

I meld my lips to hers and plunge my tongue into her mouth. The untamed flavor of Chloe hits me and I moan.

I finally have it. Everything I've ever wanted. A wife I love. A daughter I love who loves my wife.

I was afraid I lost everything today. But I fought for what I want – what I need – and I didn't give up until Chloe agreed.

I will never give up on Chloe.

Chapter 35

Ex-wife – the woman who's out to destroy your happiness but can't because her aim sucks

CHLOE

"Here you go." I hand Addy the bottle of wine for her table.

She studies me. "You're smiling."

It's true. I am. But why does she sound surprised? I smile more often. "And?"

"I've never seen you this happy."

"I've never been this happy before."

"You deserve it, Chloe." She squeezes my hand before leaving to serve her table.

"You got everything covered?" I ask the bartender. He nods and I start down the hallway toward my office.

The door to the restaurant bangs open. "Where is she? Where is the bitch who stole my husband and daughter?"

Uh oh. The ex has come a calling. I shoot off a message to Lucas to let him know Holly is at the brewery causing trouble. Technically, she hasn't caused any trouble yet, but I know her type. It's only a matter of time.

I retrace my steps to the bar. Holly is standing at the entrance swaying on her feet. Drunk as well. This should be fun.

Sophia, Nova, and Maya rush downstairs from the offices above the restaurant.

"What's going on?" Sophia asks.

Holly points at me and loses her balance. She manages to grab a chair before falling on her face. Bummer. I would love to watch her flail on the floor. I'm not going to push her but if she falls of her own accord? Not my fault.

"This b-b-bitch. She stole my husband and daughter."

"The ex-wife, I presume?" Paisley asks as she steps into the restaurant behind Holly.

"Lucas is mine." Holly pounds her chest with her free hand.

"They are legally divorced, aren't they?" Paisley asks as she passes Holly on her way to us.

"Divorced don't mean shit. Lucas is mine. All those years we were married and he never cheated on me once. He didn't have another girlfriend until you came along and stole him."

What Lucas did or didn't do during their marriage is no one's business. I motion toward a private room. "Why don't we continue this discussion in private?"

"Boo!" Addy shouts and the rest of the diners join in.

"I'm not your afternoon entertainment."

"Disagree," Judge Clara says.

Crap. The judge is here.

Sophia squeezes my hand. "It's good she's here. She'll witness how Holly acts for herself."

"But what if I can't control myself? What if I end up smacking Holly?"

"You won't." Maya squeezes my free hand. "You'll do whatever you need to do for love."

For once, I don't make fun of her obsession with romance. Because she's right. Maybe she's been right all along.

"Plus," Nova adds as she glares at Holly. "I'll punch her if she gets out of control."

"Are you feeling okay? My sunshiny, always looks on the bright side of life, friend does not punch people."

"Things have changed. This woman doesn't deserve to be a mother." Her hand dips to her stomach.

What is going on with her? I open my mouth to ask but the door opens and my personal nightmare steps inside. Is this my penance for saying I've never been happier?

"Well, well, well. I'm not surprised Chloe is causing problems. She does enjoy being troublesome."

My hands fist and I inhale a deep breath before I punch my mother in her perfect nose she needed two surgeries to perfect.

"What are you doing here?"

"I'm here with my friend."

"Holly is your friend? You don't have female friends."

"Friend. Associate. Same thing."

It's not. Your friends deserve loyalty. A trait my mother doesn't find worthy of her attention.

"She's the one who told me your marriage is fake," Holly spits out.

I glance at the judge who is now scribbling notes on a napkin. Damnit.

"My marriage to Lucas isn't fake."

Mom snorts. "Oh, please. You marry a man with a daughter? You promised you'd never have children."

Because I didn't want to become her. I rake my gaze over my mother. She's wearing form fitting red pants and matching red high heels with a white sheer blouse. Her hair – the same shade as mine – is pulled into a French twist and her lips are painted the same shade of red as her pants.

She's made up to perfection. I glance down at my simple black pants and *Five Fathoms Brewery* polo shirt. We're nothing alike.

"How much did Holly pay you for inside information on your daughter?"

Mom doesn't answer but Holly doesn't hesitate. "Five-thousand dollars and it was worth every penny."

Why did I ever worry about becoming my mother? I would never sell secrets of a friend or family for my own benefit. But Mom didn't hesitate.

"You wasted your money. You can't have Natalia, Holly."

"Natalia is my daughter!" she shrieks. "You're the one who can't have her."

"I won't let you steal her away from her father."

"It's not stealing when the judge gives me custody after he finds out your marriage to Lucas is fake."

I peek at Judge Clara. She can't find out my marriage to Lucas started out as an arrangement. She can't give custody of Natalia to Holly. I won't allow it.

"I love Lucas. He's mine now. Go find your own man."

"Lucas is my man!" Holly picks up the chair she was using to balance herself and throws it in my direction. It lands on the floor and breaks into pieces.

But Holly isn't deterred. She picks up another chair and hurls it.

"I am done with this shit," Sophia mutters before stomping forward.

I shackle her wrist. "Don't. She'll hurt you."

The door flies open and Lucas and Weston burst inside. Weston rushes to Holly.

"Don't touch me! I wasn't doing anything wrong!" Holly fights him but he doesn't have any trouble cuffing her. He leads her toward the door as he reads her, her rights.

Lucas prowls toward me. "Are you okay? Did she hurt you?" He growls. "Did she touch you?"

"I'm okay. She was a bitch, but she didn't hurt me."

He glances at the broken chairs on the floor. "What happened here?"

"She threw them at me."

His gaze sharpens. "You certain you aren't hurt?" He pinches my chin and tilts my head back. "She didn't hit you?"

I grasp his hand. "I promise she didn't hurt me."

"Thank fuck." He wraps his arms around me and I fall into him.

"No wonder there's all this fuss," Mom says.

I groan. "I guess I better introduce you to my mom."

"Not interested. She's nothing to you or us."

"Don't you worry," Mom purrs. "I promise you'll enjoy me more than my hand me downs."

I groan. I knew it. I knew my mother would hit on him.

"Not interested." Lucas smiles down at me. "I have all I need in my arms."

"Pardon me?" Mom screeches.

"I got this." Sophia grasps her hand and starts to drag her away. "I've been waiting forever to give Chloe's mother a piece of my mind."

I sigh. I don't want to speak to my mom but I can't let my friends handle this. "I'll be there in a minute."

Sophia halts. "No, you won't. You've dealt with this bitch long enough."

Mom tries to pull out of Sophia's hold. "I'm not a bitch."

Nova snorts. "Even I think you're a bitch."

"Let's go." Sophia hauls Mom away.

"No physical violence," Lucas hollers after her.

"We'll make certain," Nova says as she hurries after Sophia with Maya and Paisley on her heels.

"Ahem." Judge Clara clears her throat.

I pull away from Lucas but he wraps an arm around me to keep me close. "I'm sorry, Judge Clara. I should have insisted Holly leave the establishment. You shouldn't have been forced to witness the whole scene."

"Judge Clara?" Lucas asks. "This is the judge for our custody case?" I nod and he smiles before offering her a hand. "My wife told me about you."

"The sports day incident?" She frowns. "Will no one forget I threw a bedpan at my parents at the hospital?"

"I didn't tell him that part," I say.

Her cheeks darken. "Ah, well. Someone was bound to eventually."

"What can we do for you, your honor?" Lucas asks.

"I shouldn't be speaking to you about the case," she begins. "But between the three of us, I wouldn't worry about your fake marriage thing. It's clear you love each other."

"How could I not love this woman?" Lucas smiles down at me. "My wife is easy to love."

I snort. "Not really but this big guy is easy to love. Especially in this uniform."

Judge Clara rakes her gaze over Lucas. "I understand the attraction." Attorney Ezra motions her over to their table. "I must be going. I'll see you in court."

"Thank you for speaking to us," I say before she can leave.

"I can't remember what we spoke about." She winks before walking away.

Weston enters the bar and waves to Lucas. "I need to go. Are you sure you're okay?"

I push him away. "I'm fine. No, I'm more than fine. The judge is on our side and your ex is cuffed in the back of a police vehicle. Christmas came early this year."

"You're crazy, wildcat."

I push up on my toes to kiss him. "Love you, too, hubby. Get to work. I'll see you at home tonight."

I watch him leave with a smile on my face. I'm the luckiest woman alive. The man I love, loves me back and his ex-wife is no longer a problem.

I should plan a celebration. Just as soon as I take care of my mother.

Chapter 36

Bargain – impossible to do when you're the one behind bars

LUCAS

Weston stops me outside of the brewery. "You okay?"

I smile, remembering Chloe telling me she loves me. Hearing those words from her will never get old. "I'm good."

"You sure? Your ex just tried to assault your wife."

My good mood evaporates. "Don't remind me."

He motions to our vehicle. "There's a very mouthy reminder in our squad car."

I step toward it but he places a hand on my chest to stop me again. "I'm serious, bro. If you can't handle this professionally, I'll have you replaced."

He's right. I need to be professional. I inhale a couple of deep breaths. My anger isn't gone but it's on a low simmer now and no longer boiling.

"I'm good."

"I'm trusting you here."

"All good, bro. Swear it."

He pats me on the shoulder before leading the way to the squad car. Before we reach it, I can already hear Holly screaming.

"Let me out of here!"

Weston grins. "You leveled up with your second wife."

"Fuck yeah, I did."

"The men are falling faster than flies on Smuggler's Hideaway. First, my best friend falls in love with my little sister. And now my partner falls for the wild child of the island."

I scowl. "Chloe isn't a wild child."

He waggles his eyebrows. "Because you tamed her?"

There is no taming Chloe.

Holly bangs on the window with her cuffs. "Let me out!"

I open the front passenger door and slide into the car. "You'll get out when we reach the station."

"Lucas," she sighs. "I didn't do anything wrong."

"This should be fun," Weston mutters as he switches on the vehicle. "What do you think? Lights and sirens?"

"Lights and sirens?" Holly screeches. "I'm not a criminal! Everyone in town will see me."

"Not as stupid as she looks," Weston says.

"I'm not stupid at all! This is police harassment. I'll have your badge."

"I'm…"

Weston holds up a hand to stop me. "If you apologize for her, I'll deck you."

I chuckle. "Deck me? I'd like to see you try."

I've got five inches and a good twenty-five pounds on him.

"You're on. There's a boxing gym in Rogue's Landing. They have a ring."

"I can't believe this!" Holly yells. "I'm being harassed and you're worried about a boxing match. What happened to us?"

"I was a fucking idiot who should have got rid of your ass the first time I came home to find Natalia in a dirty diaper."

"Big deal. Her diaper was dirty. Put a clean one on her and she'd just dirty it again."

I fist my hands and ignore her for the rest of the drive. I promised Weston I'd be professional. And I will be.

"I'll book her," Weston says when we arrive. "You start the paperwork."

I hate paperwork, but I'll gladly do all the mindless paperwork to get away from my ex. I exit the car and leave him to it.

"Don't abandon me, Lucas!" Holly hollers after me but I ignore her. Her pleas mean nothing to me. The only feeling I experience when I consider her is regret.

My phone rings as I enter the station. I check the display. ***Mom calling.***

"Hey, Mom," I answer.

"Lucas, sweetheart, how are you doing? We haven't heard from you since Natalia's sports day. Which we would have come to if we had known about it. We miss our granddaughter."

I sigh. "Now's not a good time to make me feel guilty, Mom. I feel bad enough."

"Why? What's going on? I'll get your father."

"You don't need to—"

"Lucas! Come to the phone. Our son needs us."

"I'm right here, Florence. There's no need to shout."

"How do I put this dang thing on speaker?"

"Push the speaker button."

"Which one is the speaker button?"

"It says speaker on it."

"I don't have my glasses. I can't read those tiny letters."

The phone clicks.

"Hello? Are you there?"

"I'm still here, Mom."

"What's going on, son?"

"Holly's here," I begin before explaining the events of the past week.

"Why didn't you tell us before?" Mom asks.

"We could have come down there," Dad adds.

"I want you to visit when there's a reason to celebrate. Not because Holly lost her mind when she found out I remarried."

"Remarried?" Mom asks. "You didn't mention a wife."

"Why didn't you invite us to the wedding? You're too old to elope, son."

I rub a hand over my beard. Shit. I wasn't planning on telling them about my arrangement with Chloe. Hold on. There is no arrangement any longer. She is my wife.

"Why don't you come and visit now?" I ask. "Chloe would love to meet you."

"Her name is Chloe? I love her already."

"She's the best, Mom."

"I know she is. You sound happy when you say her name."

"Pack the car, Lucas. We're going to Smuggler's Hideaway."

They begin discussing how many hours the drive is. I try to interrupt them but they hang up the phone.

I can't wait for them to meet Chloe. But I have one thing I need to handle before they arrive.

Weston shakes his head when I reach the holding cells.

"Not a good idea, Lucas."

"I don't have any keys. I'm only going to speak to her."

He crosses his arms over his chest and blocks my way. "Not a good idea."

"You can listen in."

His eyes sparkle with interest. I knew they would. He loves to gossip. And getting the scoop on his partner's nasty ex-wife would be a coup for him.

He motions down the hallway. "You may proceed."

I chuckle. "I thought so."

"Lucas, you're here." Holly smiles at me. "I knew you wouldn't leave me to rot in here."

Which gives me a great idea. I know how to get rid of her.

"I have a deal for you."

She licks her lips and leans on the bars as close to me as possible. I retreat a step. I don't want her touching me. "What deal?"

"You leave town—"

"I won't be kicked out—"

I hold up a hand. "Hear me out."

She purses her lips. "Fine."

"If you agree to leave town and not return, the owners of the brewery will drop the charges against you."

I don't have Chloe and her friends' permission to offer this deal but they won't be hard to persuade.

"Drop the charges! What charges are against me? I didn't do nothing wrong."

I cross my arms over my chest and glare at her. "This is the deal they're offering."

"But if I leave town, I'll miss the custody hearing."

Which is the entire idea.

"The custody hearing is a waste of time anyway."

"Waste of time?" She hisses. "Getting custody of my daughter isn't a waste of time."

"Except you don't care about Natalia. You want custody to get child support so you don't have to work."

"Child support is only fair if I have to raise our child alone."

She won't be raising *my* daughter.

"Do you know who was in the restaurant this afternoon?" I ask.

"The slut you're pretending to be married to."

I growl and step forward. Weston clears his throat and I stop. I force my anger down. As satisfying as wringing Holly's neck might be, it won't solve the problem.

"The judge for the custody hearing," I tell her.

She pales. "The judge?"

"Yep."

"How do you know who the judge is?"

"My lawyer, who was also at the restaurant, pointed her out to me."

"Your lawyer?"

"Yep. I probably have to pay for his lunch seeing as it became a business lunch, but it's a small price to pay."

"There must be more judges on this stupid island."

"Actually," Weston interrupts. "There are but Judge Clara is the juvenile court judge."

"You couldn't have chosen a better time or place to have your little hissy fit."

She scowls. "A couple of chairs broke. It's not a big deal."

"If you don't accept this deal, you'll be charged with attempted assault. In addition to spending time in jail, the owners of the brewery could start a civil suit to have you pay for replacing the chairs."

"Take the deal," Weston says. "Considering how many people saw you attempt to assault his wife, you'll probably end up with the maximum time in jail."

Holly studies my face. If she thinks I'll be lenient because she's the mother of my child, she doesn't know me at all. She tried to injure my wife. She's lucky I was with Weston when the call came in or who knows how I would have responded.

No one – not even my ex – is allowed to harm my wife.

"Fine. Whatever."

"You'll take the deal?" I ask.

"I'll take the deal."

"I'll drive you off the island," Weston offers.

"Right now?"

"Right now."

"Thanks, bro."

He clasps my hand. "Whatever you need. Now, get out of here. Your wife is worried."

I hurry toward the stairs. I don't look back. Behind me is my past. My future is waiting for me at a brewery.

Chapter 37

Surprise – when you get caught with your husband's cock in your hands

---

A WEEK LATER

Chloe

"Where are we going?" I ask once we're in Lucas's truck driving away from our house.

"It's a surprise!" Natalia shouts.

I gathered it was a surprise when Lucas told me to get dressed in my favorite dress. I wasn't too keen on the idea until he changed into a pair of charcoal pants that hug his ass and a blue button-down shirt I want to rip off of him at the earliest opportunity.

"Why does Natalia know about the surprise and I don't?"

Lucas chuckles. "She doesn't know what the surprise is either."

"Yes, I do! We're going to *Hideaway Haven Resort* for dinner."

I moan. "I love the restaurant at the resort. They have the best seafood. But I don't need some fancy dinner. I'm happy to eat at *Smuggler's Cove*."

Lucas places a hand on my thigh. "I want to treat you. It's been a rough week."

"Tell me about it. My girlfriends drove my mother out of town and they wouldn't let me participate," I joke since I don't want to bring up how Natalia's mother was also driven out of town.

It's been a tough week with Natalia acting out. Refusing to get out of bed, getting in trouble at school for mouthing off to her teachers, and not doing her household chores.

I don't blame her. I know how it feels to have a mother who doesn't want you. I've let her be bratty all week.

But then Lucas pulled me aside and explained how I'm not helping matters. Natalia needs discipline and boundaries, he claimed. This is what I get for marrying a policeman.

"I'm glad," Lucas says. "I would have hated to arrest you."

"But you would have anyway, Mr. Stickler For The Rules."

"Rules are there for a reason."

I shake my head. "I had to fall in love with a lawman."

"You love my dad, Clo-Clo?" Natalia asks.

Oops. I guess the mermaid's out of the water.

"I do."

"And I love, Chloe," Lucas adds.

"Good. Now I don't have to worry about her leaving."

I turn to face her. "You never have to worry about me leaving. No matter what happens between me and your dad."

Lucas growls. "Nothing's happening."

I roll my eyes. "Whatever happens, you can count on me. I will always be there for you. Although, I may avoid sitting next to you on rollercoasters for the foreseeable future. I love you, sweetie. I'm not going anywhere."

"Thanks, Clo-Clo. I love you, too."

"You're lucky we're driving. Otherwise, I'd hug you on the street and embarrass you."

She giggles. "You're crazy."

"And dang proud of it, too."

Lucas turns into the entrance of *Hideaway Haven Resort*.

"It's crowded. I hope you reserved."

"I made a reservation." He finds a spot and parks. "Wait for me," he orders when I reach for the door handle.

Far be it for me to protest when my husband wants to open my door for me. He offers me his hand and helps me down. Natalia jumps to the ground next to us.

Lucas squeezes my hand. "Don't be mad."

"Why would I be mad? What did you do? Did you not reserve after all? Did I get all dressed up for nothing?"

His gaze rakes over my body. "No matter what, you didn't get dressed up for nothing," he grumbles.

I bat my eyelashes. "You like my dress?"

"I'll like it even more when it's on our bedroom floor."

I shiver. I am down with this idea. We haven't had sex in over a week since Natalia has been creeping into our bed every night.

"Surprise," he mutters and opens the door.

My jaw opens at the sight that greets me. All of my friends are here.

"Piper!" Natalia shouts and tugs on Lucas's sleeve. "Can I go say hi?"

"Go ahead, cupcake."

I wait until she's out of hearing range to ask. "What's going on?"

"We're celebrating our marriage."

"But we already had a wedding and a reception. At this very resort, in fact."

He places a hand on my lower back and steers me toward an empty alcove. "Wildcat," he says and draws me into his arms. "I want a real celebration. Not the fake one we had when we got married."

"I don't know. Our first kiss felt awful real. Not to mention how sexy our first dance was."

He frames my face with his hands. "I love you, Chloe Fellows. I want to celebrate our love. I'd give you another wedding if I could but you'll have to settle for a wedding night do over."

"I hope you got the cabin with the hot tub on the deck. We're going in there naked."

He moans. "Do not make me hard when I have to greet my friends and family."

I sneak my hand through our bodies to find his hard cock and squeeze it. "I could take care of your little problem now before the party."

"Little problem?"

"Lucas Fellows! You bring us your bride this moment or I'm going to lose patience," a woman shouts.

"Listen to your mother, son," a man answers.

"Son?" My pulse increases until I can barely breathe. "Your parents are here?"

"They can't wait to meet you."

I drop my hand. I do not want to be caught with his cock in my hand when I meet his parents.

"You could have told me they'd be here."

He brushes the hair from my face. "It's a surprise, remember?" He kisses my nose and grasps my hand. "Let's go meet them."

I tug on his hand. "What if they don't like me?"

"Wildcat, do you love me?" I nod. "Do you love my daughter?" I nod again. "Then, they're going to love you, too."

I don't understand his reasoning but I allow him to lead me to the foyer where an elderly couple is waiting.

"Mom, Dad, this is Chloe."

"I love her already," his mom squeals before rushing me and throwing her arms around me. "Welcome to the family. I'm sorry we weren't at the wedding." She pulls back to glare at her son. "But someone didn't tell us."

His dad claps Lucas on the back. "You're a bit old to keep secrets from your parents."

"It's my fault," I say. "I don't have any parents and I was intimidated to meet you. Don't blame him. Lucas didn't do anything wrong. He's perfect."

His dad smiles. "She's perfect for you, son."

"I am nowhere near perfect. We should get this straight from the start before you set high expectations I can't meet, Mr. Fellows."

He chuckles. "Mr. Fellows? We're family. You can call me Lucas. Or, if you want, Dad."

"Dad?" My bottom lip trembles and my eyes get itchy. "I've never had a dad before."

He kisses my cheek. "You do now, sweetheart."

A tear escapes and Lucas wipes it away. "Don't cry, wildcat."

"These are happy tears. I'll cry if I want to."

He palms my cheeks. "And here I was worried you'd be mad at me."

I slap his shoulder. "Why would I be mad? Do you not want your parents to like me?"

"I have a girl crush," his mom says and I focus my gaze on her. "What? Did I say that wrong? I saw it on the tickety-tock."

"The tickety-tock?" I giggle. "I think I have a girl crush on you, too, Mrs. Fellows."

"You can call me Florence or Flo. Or maybe Mama Flo. Is it cool sounding?"

I beam at her. "Mama Flo it is."

"Shall we join the party?" Lucas ask and motions toward the room where we had our wedding reception.

His parents go ahead of us as we walk to the ballroom.

"How many people did you invite?" I ask him when we enter.

"Everyone who was at our wedding, plus my parents."

"You didn't need to do this."

"I love you, wildcat. I want to give you everything you want even if you didn't realize you wanted it."

"You're good at this."

"I learned from the best." He nods to his parents. His dad hands his mom a drink before offering her a chair.

"I lucked out when you moved in next door."

"Nah, wildcat. I'm the lucky one."

I push up on my tiptoes to kiss him. He palms my neck and pulls me close until our lips meet. I groan at the taste of him. Lucas's flavor of musk and man is addicting. I sigh and he pushes his tongue inside. My tongue reaches out to duel with his.

"You're pregnant! Who the fuck is the father?" Hudson shouts and I break up our kiss.

Lucas's brow wrinkles. "What's going on?"

I grin. "I don't know but let's go find out."

I clasp his hand and lead him toward the table where Nova is sitting. She's throwing daggers from her eyes at Hudson. If they were real, he'd be bleeding out on the floor and Lucas would have to arrest one of my best friends at our wedding reception re-do party.

"Life is never going to be boring with you around," Lucas says.

"Get your seatbelt strapped on and hold on for the ride!"

Chapter 38

Nova – a woman who thinks she's been keeping a secret from her friends

NOVA

"I don't know why this party has to be at *Hideaway Haven Resort*," I complain as I drive Maya and Paisley toward the resort where Lucas has set up a surprise party for Chloe.

"I think it's romantic," Maya says. "They're having a do-over of their wedding reception, but this time they're in love."

"I'm just glad the resort is now carrying our beer," Paisley says. "Good job on landing the account, Nova."

My cheeks heat when I remember how I landed the account. My methods weren't part of any business class I attended in college. I glance down at my belly. And I wouldn't recommend them.

"Does this mean you get to see more of the sexy owner of the resort?" Maya asks.

I scowl. "I don't want to see Hudson any more than I already do."

"But you never see him."

That's not exactly true, but I am not clearing up her misconception.

"Which is exactly the way I want to keep it."

"I don't understand," Paisley says. "You clearly find the man attractive. Why don't you want to see him?"

Thank the smugglers in heaven, we've arrived at the resort because I am not answering her question. I park, switch off the engine, and jump out of the car. My stomach cramps and I place a hand over it. This is not the time to throw up. You'd think I threw up enough today already. You'd be wrong.

"What's your hurry?" Maya asks as she rounds the car to where I'm standing.

"We're supposed to be waiting in the lobby when Chloe and Lucas arrive."

Paisley checks the time. "They should be here any minute. Let's get inside."

The foyer is crowded with guests. I spot Sophia with Flynn and her brother Weston and join them.

"I can't believe Chloe is the second one of us to fall in love and the first one to get married. My money was on Maya," Sophia says.

Maya's cheeks heat. "I'm not in a hurry to find love," she whispers.

Weston smirks. "Because you're waiting for a certain someone to come home."

I elbow him. "Don't embarrass her."

He doesn't get a chance to answer before Lucas and Chloe arrive and everyone cheers.

"Awesome. The couple is here. I've greeted them. Time to go find some company for the evening." Weston wiggles his eyebrows before wandering off.

Sophia frowns. "I can't believe my brother is such a man whore."

Flynn kisses her cheek. "I'll keep an eye on him."

"Don't forget you promised to drive home," she shouts after him.

"I can drive you home if you drink too much," I offer.

She narrows her eyes at me. "Aren't you drinking?" I shake my head. "Why not?"

I can hardly tell her the real reason. I've barely acknowledged the truth myself. I shrug instead.

"Not feeling well."

She frowns but doesn't comment. My friends are used to my hypochondria. She threads her arm through my elbow. "Come on. We'll get you some seltzer water."

She leads me to the ballroom with Paisley and Maya following us.

"This is beyond romantic," Maya says when we enter.

I smile as I look around. "Agree. I'm happy Chloe found happiness."

Paisley nods. "Me too. She was very lonely."

"She wasn't lonely," I insist. "She had us. What else could she need?"

Maya points to Chloe and Lucas standing with his parents. "Him. She needed him."

Sophia sighs. "Since Chloe's found love, there's no one around to make fun of Maya's romantic tendencies."

Good. I'm glad. No one should make fun of Maya. She pretends it doesn't bother her, but I know it does. How could it not after how her parents acted?

Paisley studies the seating chart. "Our table is over there."

"Meet ya there. I'll get the drinks." Sophia skips off to the bar where Flynn happens to be.

"She's going to be a while," I mutter as I weave my way through the tables to ours. I read the nametags to find my spot. I scowl when I notice who's seated next to me. "Why is Hudson invited?"

"He's a client," Paisley says.

"It's a huge account." As the financial wizard of *Five Fathoms Brewing*, Maya is well aware of how big an account the resort is.

Which is why I pushed and pushed until Hudson agreed to give our beer a trial run. My stomach flutters. I may have pushed too hard.

"Here, we go." Sophia arrives with a bottle of champagne and four glasses.

I hold up my hand when she tries to hand a glass to me. "I'm driving."

"And she hasn't been feeling well," Maya adds.

I smile to hide how annoyed I am with her. She's not supposed to tell anyone I haven't been feeling well. Although I didn't make her promise to keep quiet. Maybe I should have.

Sophia hands me a glass of ginger ale. "Here you go, spoilsport."

"I'm not a spoilsport."

"No, she's not." Paisley points to my stomach. "She's pregnant."

I gasp. "How do you know?"

Sophia slams her glass on the table. "It's true? Why does Paisley know and I don't?"

Maya holds up her hand. "I didn't know either. I mean, I suspected. But I didn't actually know."

"You suspected?" Sophia asks.

Maya motions to me. "She's been throwing up every morning at work. Haven't you noticed?"

"I have," Paisley says. "I also noticed she hasn't been drinking. Not even champagne to celebrate our friend's marriage, which could only mean one thing."

"I'm pregnant."

"Yes." She nods. "The only question I have is who is the father of your baby."

"You're pregnant! Who the fuck is the father?" Hudson shouts, and I cringe. Where did he come from? "Were you fucking him when we were together?"

I stand to face him. "Can you please stop shouting the f-word?"

He gets in my face. "Who is the father of your baby?"

I push him away. "Do not shout in my face."

"Fuck. Sorry."

I glare at him. "Do you know any words besides the f-word?"

"Do you know who the father of your baby is?"

He can't be serious. Does he think I'm a slut? Before I know what's happening, my hand is slapping his face.

"You are, you jerk. I don't sleep around."

He captures my hand. "Let's go."

"Go? I'm not going anywhere with you."

He leans down to whisper in my ear. "Do you want to discuss how you're carrying my baby in front of the entire island?"

I scan the room. Sure enough. Everyone in the place is watching and listening. Even Chloe is making her way across the room with a smile on her face.

"Fine. We'll discuss this in private. But I don't need you to drag me." I wrench my hand from his hold.

"Follow me." He leads the way to a door marked *private*.

I wasn't planning on revealing my pregnancy to my friends let alone the father of the baby today but I no longer have a choice. I eye the patio door leading to the deck and pool area. Unless I decide to make a run for it.

Nope. I'm not a runner.

I straighten my back. I can do this. I've survived much worse.

Chapter 39

Happy ending – includes new neighbors, a dog, and love – lots and lots of love

ONE MONTH LATER

Lucas

"Chloe? Are you home, wildcat?"

When she doesn't answer, I climb the stairs to our bedroom. I shake my head at the mess of her clothes scattered around the room on the floor. I can't abide a messy home but with Chloe, I don't mind.

As long as the woman I love is living with me and sharing my bed at night, she can be as messy as she wants.

"Chloe?"

She walks out of the attached bathroom and smiles at me. "Hey. I thought you were on law and protect duty until later."

I catch her hand and haul her near. I meld my lips to hers and enjoy how she melts into my arms. How she gives herself up to the pleasure only I can offer her.

Unfortunately, I can't bend her over the bed and sink into her now. I have news. News that might give me blue balls for a while if my wildcat doesn't approve.

I pull away and she mewls. "Why did you stop?"

"We need to talk." I sit on the bed and arrange her in my lap.

"This isn't a talking position." She rubs herself over my hard length.

I dig my fingers into her hips to still her movements and my cock protests. "I'm serious, wildcat. We need to talk."

"Fine," she huffs. "What do you want to talk about?"

"You know how you gave up the lease on your house?"

She rolls her eyes. "Yes, I know *I* gave up my lease."

"There are new renters."

"I figured it wouldn't be long before new renters arrived. Finding property on Smuggler's Hideaway is tough. Ask Sophia how she ended up with Flynn sometime."

I chuckle. I've heard all about how Chloe and her friends pushed Sophia to live with Flynn while her apartment was being renovated.

I wonder what they're going to do about Nova now they know she's pregnant with Hudson's baby. I'd warn Hudson but I've seen the way he looks at Nova when no one's looking. He wants her.

"We know the renters."

Chloe perks up. "We do? Is it Nova and Hudson?"

Maybe I should warn Hudson after all.

"No. I don't know if you're going to like the new tenants."

"Won't like them? Are they teetotalers? Teetotalers and Smuggler's Hideaway is not a good combo."

"No."

"Are they—"

I place my finger over her lips before she can offer another insane suggestion.

"It's my parents."

"Your parents? As in Dad Lucas and Mama Flo?"

"Yes."

"Awesome. We're getting a dog."

Just when I think I've peeled back all the layers of her, she surprises me with another layer to reveal.

"What? I don't follow. I tell you my parents are moving in next door and your response is we're getting a dog?"

"If Dad and Mama Flo are next door, they can walk our dog if you have an emergency and have to work late or if I'm pulling a double shift at the restaurant."

I know Chloe loves my parents. But it's one thing to love your in-laws when they live several states away. It's another thing for them to live next door to you.

"That's it?"

Her brow wrinkles. "What's it?"

"You're not mad?"

"Why would I be mad? Am I supposed to be mad? Is this because you want to have make up sex? We don't have to argue to have sex."

She grabs my cock and squeezes. I moan. I grit my teeth and shackle her wrist to remove her hand. I need to make sure she's okay with this latest development before I bury myself inside her.

"You're seriously okay with my parents living next door?"

"I love your parents."

"I love them, too, but they'll be right next door to us. Mom will pop in for coffee and Dad will do our yardwork without us asking him to."

"Great. I hate yardwork."

"Wildcat, you're not hearing me."

Her nose wrinkles. "Are you trying to get me mad? Is this the make up sex thing again?"

"Your mind works in mysterious ways."

She beams. "Thank you."

"You won't mind how involved they are in our lives? Because they will be very involved."

"They'll be involved in their granddaughter's life, too. They'll be there when she has school plays or track meets. When she goes to prom, her grandparents will be there to snap pictures. I think it's great Natalia will have her grandparents close by."

Typical Chloe. She's putting Natalia before herself again. Why she ever thought she'd be a bad mother is beyond me.

"But they'll be next door and involved in our lives, too."

"Good. They can babysit Natalia whenever we want a little alone time."

I cup her cheeks. "You're really okay with this?"

"I'm more than okay with this. I love your parents and I know how to set boundaries. Everything is going to be okay. More than okay. It'll be great. We're getting a puppy."

I want to add we'll be having more children as well but I know she's not ready yet.

The front door bangs open. "Hello!" Natalia shouts. "Is anyone home?"

Chloe kisses me quick before standing. She holds out her hand to me. "Ready to give your daughter the good news?"

"Let's go."

We discover Natalia rooting around in the refrigerator. "There's nothing to eat in here."

"I'll make you a sandwich," Chloe offers but I stop her.

"Why don't we sit at the table for a family meeting first?"

"Uh oh," Chloe whisper-shouts. "Someone's in trouble."

"The school called? It's not my fault, I swear."

"What did you do?" I ask.

Chloe draws a finger across her throat, but I grasp her hand and pull her into a chair next to mine.

"We'll discuss what you did after our news."

"You're pregnant? Yes!" Natalia claps her hands. "I'm getting a sister or brother. I'll be the big sister and can boss them around. I need to phone Piper."

Chloe clutches her stomach. "I'm not pregnant."

"You're not getting a sister or brother *yet*," I add.

Chloe scowls at me before addressing Natalia. "We're getting a puppy!"

"Yippie! I've always wanted a puppy, but Dad said I couldn't get one. Can we go get one now? Where do you get puppies from anyway?"

"The puppy is not the news," I say.

Chloe ignores me. "There's an animal shelter on the mainland. We can go there."

Natalia jumps up from the table. "I'll get my shoes on."

"Wait," I order and she skids to a stop. "The puppy is not the news."

"You're not pregnant. Getting a puppy is not the news. What is the news, Dad?"

"Yeah, Dad," Chloe mimics. "What is the news?"

She'll regret teasing me later when we're in bed and I won't let her come until she's begging me. My cock twitches as I imagine her cuffed to the bed and at my mercy. I clear my throat. In front of my daughter is not the appropriate time to have sexy fantasies.

"Your grandparents are moving to Smuggler's Hideaway."

"Yeah, I know. They told me a while ago." Her eyes widen. "Wait! Are they moving in next door?"

I nod and she squeals.

"I'm going to say hi."

She rushes off and this time I let her. She's only going next door. Maybe my parents living close by is a blessing after all.

"We should go welcome your parents to the island."

I shackle Chloe's wrist before she can leave the kitchen. "We're alone now."

Her eyes flare. "We are," she breathes out.

"I'll call my parents to keep Natalia occupied for an hour. You go upstairs and get naked."

"Your parents moving in next door is the best thing ever."

I wrap my arms around her. "No. Me moving in next door to you was the best thing ever."

She melts in my arms. "I love you, Lucas."

"And I love you, wildcat." I push her away. "Now, go get naked." I pat her ass and she giggles as she runs away.

I am the luckiest man in the world.

D. E. Haggerty

Love and Laughter in Every Chapter

About the author

D.E. Haggerty is an American who has spent the majority of her adult life abroad. She has lived in Istanbul, various places throughout Germany, and currently finds herself in The Hague. She has been a military policewoman, a lawyer, a B&B owner/operator and now a writer.

Printed in Great Britain
by Amazon